galaxy
SCIENCE FICTION

GW01044327

Editor-in-Chief Justin T. O'Conor Sloane
Deputy Editor-in-Chief Jean-Paul L. Garnier
Science Editor Dr. Daniel Pomarède

Contributing Editor Robert Silverberg
Proofreader Pedro Iniguez
Design & Layout by F. J. Bergmann

Galaxy (ISSN 2995-9527 for webzine, ebook, and PDF formats and ISSN 2995-9519 and ISBN 979-8-9886342-3-2 for print format) is published periodically by Starship Sloane Publishing Company, Inc., Justin T. O'Conor Sloane, President. Main offices: Austin-Round Rock, Texas. Issue #263 PDF is free for a limited time; thereafter price per copy TBD. Annual subscription and issue count TBD: Price TBD in the United States, elsewhere TBD. Periodical Class Mail postage paid at point of publication. Copyright 2024 by Starship Sloane Publishing Company, Inc. under International, Universal and Pan-American Copyright Conventions. All rights reserved. The publisher assumes no responsibility for unsolicited material. All stories published in this magazine are works of fiction and any similarity between characters and events depicted therein, and actual persons and events, is coincidental. Title registered United States Patent and Trademark Office. Printed in the United States of America. Starship Sloane publishes a variety of books and magazines. Visit starshipsloane.com for more information. All text © the respective authors.

Opinions herein are not necessarily those of the Galaxy Science Fiction staff or Starship Sloane Publishing Company, Inc.

For fan mail please email galaxysciencefiction@gmail.com   https://galaxysf.com/

From the Editor-in-Chief

This magazine is perhaps best enjoyed with the following suggested pairings.

Playlist:
"Heartbeats," "Silent Shout" & "The Captain" by The Knife
TRST by TR/ST
"Summer in Berlin" & "Sounds Like a Melody" by Alphaville
"Computer Love," "Home Computer," "The Robots" & "Radioactivity" by Kraftwerk
Oldschool Trance Vinyl-mix HD by DJ Yilmars

Highball:
Gin and tonic (1:1, heavily squeezed lime wedge, heavy ice) ... refill often

Dear Reader,

Welcome to the relaunch of *Galaxy Science Fiction* magazine! I am very glad that you are here. This great magazine has a long and storied history. A new chapter is now being written and it is my hope that we will contribute meaningfully to this history. While I genuinely hold no pretensions in the matter, I do firmly believe that we will be successful in furthering the legacy of this venerable magazine.

Galaxy and *Worlds of IF* were long sister publications and I am delighted that they are so once more! That they are being published only months apart just adds to my sense of excitement. A symmetry in continuum has been achieved with this. What once was, is again.

I will briefly touch upon the history of *Galaxy* in this editorial, of course, as I think I would be at least somewhat remiss in my duties if I did not, but I do prefer to talk more about the here and now this go-around. (Be sure to read Robert Silverberg's essay on the early days of *Galaxy*, right here in this issue!)

I have already written my most pressing thoughts concerning the passage of time, a community of shared culture, a sense of nostalgia, my perception of continuum, SF magazine history in general and the important things that I view science fiction as bringing to the collective table of thought and literature in my editorial for the debut issue of *Worlds of IF*—which is still available to read, free of charge, at **worldsofifmagazine.com** (and here's the inside scoop: that issue will remain free to read, indefinitely, a gift to the science fiction community). I am fairly certain that you know much about this influential magazine already—if not, Bob's essay will bring you up to something approaching light speed in the matter.

Now, speaking of that history, hats off to the illustrious H. L. Gold and his tremendous accomplishments as the editor extraordinaire of this magazine, and further, in helping to shape and define the field of science fiction itself. His contributions are still felt today. Very much so. The founding of *Galaxy* is often incorrectly attributed to him (the magazine was in fact founded by the French-Italian publisher World Editions and established in Boston), however, he was its first editor. Vera Cerutti was the editor-in-chief and had approached Gold about coming on board. Vera Cerutti is, surprisingly enough, rarely mentioned in discussions about *Galaxy* and given even less credit, yet she was an instrumental force in developing the magazine from its inception and should be better associated with its subsequent success. She was an early female pioneer in what was a male-dominated industry and so I would venture that is a reason for her contributions to *Galaxy* having been largely relegated to peripheral mentions—and once written out, it's difficult to be written back in. She knew that Gold had the talent to make *Galaxy* a winner—she was quite right—and the rest, as they say, is history. A brilliant one. As well, hats off to the phenomenal editors later in *Galaxy*'s history, like Frederik Pohl, who immediately comes to mind and who also did a smash-up job with *Worlds of IF*, earning it three straight Hugos for best pro mag.

It is my hope that a professional magazine, skinny, published on a regular yet infrequent schedule and containing the work of outrageously talented people, will be a successful model for longevity and at least some degree of profitability. My publishing model for *Worlds of IF* is semi-pro and bulky in comparison, intent on steadily gaining more weight and, aspirationally, to be published more often. (Will either ever achieve a regular publishing schedule? Maybe, maybe not.) We'll see which approach works better. And adjustments will be made. The publishing industry can be a tough nut to crack. I hope to see science fiction magazines flourishing in the great quantity of selection that they once did. Newsstands—physical or digital—spilling forth with SF magazines! A pipe dream perhaps, but when *Amazing Stories* popped back into view from behind a long, gray cloud of oblivion, I celebrated. (See Deputy EIC Jean-Paul L. Garnier's interview with *Amazing*'s editor, Lloyd Penney, at **worldsofifmagazine.com**.) Their reemergence from the void is in part what inspired me to revive *Galaxy* and *Worlds of IF*. I hope that many more will return. If these magazines can serve as a source of inspiration for others to do the same, then I would consider that to be a public good. Or, this may end up becoming a cautionary tale. Either way, I will be happy to have tried. Go big or go home is my mantra, and it's one that I would recommend to anybody who desires that their dreams should actually take flight, soaring into the vast expanse of the possible on supercharged wings of an almost otherworldly provenance. Early on, Jean-Paul had said to me that I needed to be realistic (something that I try to avoid if at all possible) about the challenges facing publishers; he was right, of course, but it is going well enough, and I am very thankful for that. Anyway, I hope that the long-term results will be of note and perhaps even profitable. That's the goal. A robust sustainability. That this relaunched magazine should stick around for a good, long while—a significant run that will add measurably to its storied legacy.

I think that we are off to a great start! From the front cover to the back cover, this magazine hits on all cylinders. With a feature story by David Gerrold leading the way, all of the stories and poetry are new and the art is splendid. (Fear not! Each future issue will include a reprint of a Robert Silverberg story, selected by the guy who wrote it.) The cover art, the extraordinary *Fungus Gigantica* (1990) by Bruce Pennington, is a private work that appeared in the book *Ultraterranium: The Paintings of Bruce Pennington* by Nigel Suckling (Paper Tiger, 1992). It is exceptional, dazzling science fiction art, presenting the very vision of science fiction imagery that has thunderwelled my mind into orbit since I was but a wee lad! Even the title is pure SF gold. And this piece has not been cover art before, either, which is a very nice touch for this relaunch. Bruce is one of the greatest SF&F artists of all time, and another of his works of art will grace the cover of the third issue of *Worlds of IF* as well. The magnificent back cover art by Paulo Sayeg exerts a field of such transfixing gravity that it should come with a warning as you may find yourself being pulled inexorably into the page, chair and all, but you won't mind one bit. With literary work in this issue by Bacon, Bergmann, Boey, Dalton, Evtimova, Gerrold, Powell, and Ruocchio, you will be treated to high-voltage writing by some seriously dangerous talent. *Galaxy* lives again—and it's electric!

Also, as is usually so with Starship Sloane magazines, this is an international affair, with contributors from Australia, Brazil, Bulgaria, France, Singapore, the UK and of course, these (arguably) United States.

A quick note here. Following her most recent novel, *He May Wear My Silence*, published by Starship Sloane, Zdravka Evtimova has provided another story, "You Recognized Her," that seems to go beyond geoscience fiction into something more akin to what I would term geoanimistic science fiction. Zdravka's work always makes my brain do somersaults and this story is no exception. Animate landscapes have an interesting and ancient history, one that is particularly evident in the spiritual traditions of Tibet and the Far East. I think that she is blazing a unique path in science fiction with this thematic exploration. You be the Occidental judge. It's interesting stuff.

I very much appreciate that the talented editorial team from *Worlds of IF* is back on board for Starship Sloane Publishing's relaunch of *Galaxy*! Jean-Paul L. Garnier is reprising his role as deputy editor-in-chief, Dr. Daniel Pomarède as science editor, Robert Silverberg as contributing editor, and F.

J. Bergmann as design and layout guru. On that note, congratulations to F. J. for winning the SFPA Grand Master Award this year! She joins the likes of Ray Bradbury in having received this significant distinction, recognition for her distinguished body of work. I'm pleased to also announce the addition of speculative poet Pedro Iniguez as proofreader. What a team, and I value them greatly! As I mentioned in my editorial for *Worlds of IF*, bringing together talented people who share a vision is the key to building a foundation for success and sustainability. Daniel is one of the world's foremost cosmographers, having co-discovered utterly mind-blowing cosmic structures, galactic superclusters, voids, and a BAO. (Be sure to read Daniel's positively remarkable essay on baryon acoustic oscillations in this issue!) While Jean-Paul has been described as "one of the seminal figures in the modern speculative landscape" by *Radon Journal*. Bob really needs no introduction, as it would be, I think, inconceivable for a fan of science fiction to not be familiar with his absolutely stellar body of award-winning work that spans decades, eras, and generations. It is a privilege and an almost hallucinogenic honor to collaborate creatively with such expansively talented folks in the field of science fiction.

I would also like to take a moment to state my genuine appreciation to some very special contributors whose wonderful work has graced the various publications of Starship Sloane Publishing over the years prior to launching these higher-profile mags and who have honored me once again with their involvement in this one. I owe them a debt of gratitude. Importantly, they have helped me to build an overall momentum that has energized a certain confidence and sense of inspired resolve in undertaking these larger projects. Going in alphabetical order, thank you: F. J. Bergmann, Ronan Cahill, Bob Eggleton, Zdravka Evtimova, Jean-Paul L. Garnier, Richard Grieco, Rodney Matthews, Bruce Pennington, Dr. Daniel Pomarède, Paulo Sayeg, Nigel Suckling, and Dave Vescio. Thank you for your contributions to science fiction!

Special thanks to Robert Silverberg for being a really great sport about completing the very lengthy and undoubtedly groan-inducing interview that you will find anchoring this issue after the stories, poetry, and art have sailed you across a broad expanse of the cosmic imagination and back again. It was my intention that this should be a fairly definitive interview with a legend of science fiction. I think it succeeds in being that. It is a delightful interview that is brimming with insight, wisdom, and perspective. I enjoyed the interview and learned much; I hope that you do as well. *Galaxy*, like *Worlds of IF*, is another SF homecoming of sorts for Bob. I appreciate his recollections and knowledge, his insight, and his enthusiasm for this magazine and *Worlds of IF*. Regarding his role as contributing editor with the magazines, he stated that it's a strange business being a link between generations and a bridge between distinct eras of science fiction. I would imagine so. When I decided to commit to relaunching these magazines, the vision that they should draw deeply upon their history while also charting a new course in writing the new chapters of that history was a driving force in my thinking. To build a new and unique architecture upon an existing—and at times, repurposed—foundation. A living architecture. In this context, Bob provides an instrumental voice in connecting the old with the new, that which has already been built with that which is being built, residing in both spaces, facilitating in the expression of that vision. In a sense, he is the keystone in this particular arch of the vision.

Special thanks to Bruce Pennington for granting me an interview. Interviews are not at the top of his list particularly and so I consider it to be a stroke of luck to have gotten this one. Bruce's generosity in permitting Starship Sloane Publishing to present his brilliant artwork in its various magazines over the years has been exceptional and very much appreciated. I've written at length about Bruce's work and its influence on me (see *The Flying Saucer Poetry Review* #2 for more on this), so I'll keep it brief this time around. Suffice it to say that Bruce's work is unequivocally among the very best and most influential out there and is a top favorite of mine. As we do in fact judge books by their cover (and I think that we should), I would venture to say that Bruce's cover art for the *Dune* series by Frank Herbert caught eyes by the netsful, furthering it along in becoming one of the all-time bestselling science fiction series in the world. In the interview, Bruce provides what I consider to be the best advice I've heard regarding the approach that any aspiring science fiction & fantasy artist would be wise to implement in their journey to professional, artistic success.

David Gerrold is one of the greats of science fiction, and I am absolutely delighted to present the first three chapters of his soon-to-be-released novella, *Praxis*, as this issue's feature story! I have written in other editorials that *Star Trek* was the first television show I ever watched and is one of the reasons that the word "starship" is in the title of this publishing house—Gene Roddenberry just might be its patron saint. David's work on the show—and far beyond, of course—is legendary. He has won the big SF awards in a career spanning many decades, and he continues to write exciting stories with a riveting level of sophistication. His stories importantly reflect and process today's social and political zeitgeist as seamlessly and effectively as they did in the '60s and '70s and in each decade since. *Praxis* is page-turning reading and I think that David's nuanced exploration of the social, emotional, and very personal mechanics of human preparation for colonizing other worlds is moving and original in its presentation. It is a deeply compelling treatment of the intrapersonal landscape and of the growth required to arrive at the genuinely authentic and productive interpersonal relationships necessary for navigating survival on an alien world. Work that in with hard science fiction and you have a combination that would make both Gold and Campbell very happy indeed. I hope that you enjoy the three-chapter excerpt.

I am also thrilled to announce that Starship Sloane will publish the entirety of *Praxis* in the near future—with an absolutely pitch-perfect and beautifully articulated foreword by John Shirley and a gorgeous cover art commission by Bob Eggleton. Please stay tuned for the release!

And now, good people of science fiction, here is a mystery teaser of sorts! In exciting news that I'm going to be annoyingly secretive about, a batch of never-before-published stories belonging to a well-known series will begin appearing in the second issue of *Worlds of IF*, which I think SF fans will be very excited about. I made the decision to publish the stories in *Worlds of IF* as I think that when taken from the perspective of the historical, editorial approach of each magazine it is a better fit. There is an interesting backstory to these stories, to be told by the gentleman who spent years in search of them, which will be told in installments to accompany each story when published. There is also an interesting and historical context which I will provide as an editor's note at the time of publication. There is a remote possibility that I will also publish some of the stories in *Galaxy* if my enthusiasm for them completely overrides my initial thinking in the matter, but that would also require having to revisit the rights granted to Starship Sloane Publishing, which I prefer not to do. So, we will see, but do stay tuned! This will conclude a story of lost stories and push the series itself out to something approaching 100 years— an ideal complement to the conceptual energy, the sense of continuum, behind the relaunch of these magazines.

A final note. Work submitted to *Galaxy* and *Worlds of IF* is currently by invitation only and subscriptions to the magazines are not yet available, if they ever will be. If there is a change in either, that information will be communicated via the websites, email updates, and social media. I will also add this information to the website of each magazine, as I am asked questions about both on an almost daily basis. You can still sign up at each website for email updates, but for the time being, I have closed the email portals and various social media comms, as I simply cannot keep up with the volume of inquiries. I genuinely appreciate the interest, though!

Some closing thoughts. Now, more than ever, science fiction has become science fact in the world we inhabit. The genre is more relevant today than it has ever been. I think that this state of being infuses science fiction with an energy of excitement and an intensity of the possible that has taken it to a whole new level. I also think that people are less likely to dismiss the ideas presented by science fiction outright, even when seemingly fanciful. The human imagination, expressed in the form of science fiction, has proven itself to be prescient, remarkably so. Some might even argue, preternaturally so. In divining the future, science fiction has also defined it. In its limitless creativity, there is no field of thought that I would rather be associated with.

We ride this generation starship together into a future that is both known and unknown all at once, as we will write that future in part. Science fiction has rightly been called the literature of ideas. It provides humanity with a living blueprint of possible futures, reflecting boundless ideas, civilization-scale experiments and world-building that we may add to, tinker with, choose from and leverage in constructing the glowing edifice of a bright tomorrow.

And so, here we are. Can you believe it? *Galaxy* is back! The coolest stuff always comes around again—magazines being no exception.

Enjoy the poetry, flash, short stories, essays, art and the interviews in this debut issue of *Galaxy Science Fiction* magazine!

Thank you to everyone who has made this debut possible and thank you for reading!

Safe travels, children of the stars …

Cheers,
Justin T. O'Conor Sloane,
Austin-Round Rock Metro, TX
June 30, 2024

Mulher Gavião 2 by Paulo Sayeg

From the Deputy Editor-in-Chief

First *Worlds of IF*, and now *Galaxy*! It makes perfect sense to me, because SF today is so rich and full of wonderful stories from all over the world. It's been an honor to work with all of the talented authors that fill these pages. Reading these stories and poetry has solidified my belief that SF is in a constant state of flux, bringing with it great variety, and that together our voices crying out to the stars will be heard. It comes as no surprise that SF keeps evolving, as does science, and our species, both collectively and as individuals. The world is seeing many dark days in the 21st century, but it is also filled with cries of hope, defiance, and human expression. The things that make life, and fiction, worthwhile.

All of the text that fills these pages is appearing for the first time. One of the great honors of being an editor is to read works that no one else has yet read, and help to bring them into the world for others to enjoy. I'd like to thank all of the authors for trusting us with their amazing work, and all of our readers, I know that you are in for a treat. So, sit back and enjoy the incredible rides that these authors are about to take you on.

Jean-Paul L. Garnier,
Joshua Tree, CA
2024

The Musée Mercurius by Bruce Pennington

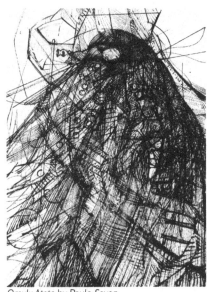

Omulu Atoto by Paulo Sayeg

From the Science Editor

From Deep Darkness Came Murmurs of Awakening

Dr. Daniel Pomarède

In the first 380,000 years after its birth, the Big Bang universe was a hot cauldron where two antagonistic forces fought each other—a titanic duel, from which grew the current large-scale structure in the distribution of matter that we are part of, including our galaxy. Back then, plasma filled the universe: the primordial plasma, a soup of charged particles, electrons and protons. And there was light; that is, photons, scattering on these particles. Along with the ordinary matter that made this plasma—that cosmologists refer to as baryonic matter—another component would play an important role: dark matter. Indeed, earlier, in the very first fraction of a second of the Big Bang, during this phase of rapid expansion called the inflation, random quantum fluctuations created inhomogeneities throughout the entire universe, creating a patchwork of underdense and overdense regions. Dark matter accumulated in overdense hotspots; cosmic voids developed in underdense coldspots.

The scene of the cosmic battlefield is now set up and the fight begins between the two opponents: gravitation versus pressure. On one side, dark-matter clumps attract their surroundings through the gravitational force. The plasma collapses onto these clumps. As a result, the pressure of the plasma increases; it reacts by pushing against the dark matter's gravitation. Dark matter pulls back, and the system enters into an oscillating state, which, like a drum, generate spherical sound waves, emanating from the clumps, and propagating through the plasma. These are the so-called BAOs (baryon acoustic oscillations), relativistic sound waves, that travelled at 57% of the speed of light. These primordial waves propagated until the universe was 380,000 years old, at which point the universe had become cold enough that the first atoms could form. As a result, the plasma vanished, but on the wavefront of the frozen waves, there would remain an overdensity in the distribution of matter, where the formation of galaxies would be enhanced.

9

Theorists predicted the emergence of BAOs in 1970, but it was only in 2005 that the imprint of BAOs was discovered by analyzing large catalogs of galaxies, where there appears a peak, that is, a favored value, in the distance separating pairs of any two galaxies. This discovery had important consequences in cosmology: indeed, all of the BAO spherical waves were frozen at the same time, all reaching the same diameter, of 1 billion light-years. By measuring the present diameter of these shells, one can infer the expansion rate of the universe, that is, the value of the Hubble constant, one of the most important parameters of the Standard Model of Cosmology. Then, one year ago, in 2023, 53 years after their prediction, we discovered a cosmological structure that we posited is the remnant of an individual BAO. This serendipitous discovery came as a surprise, because the BAOs are considered very difficult to detect individually. Indeed, these spherical sound waves were created throughout the entire universe, overlapping one with another so as to form a quasi-continuous background. By analogy, it's like raindrops falling on the still surface of a lake: if there is only one drop, one will see the concentric ring pattern of the waves it creates, whereas when an entire rainfall pours onto the lake, the many ring-like waveforms overlap one with another so that one can't distinguish them anymore. The structure we found in the distribution of galaxies appears as a spherical shell, 1 billion light-years in diameter. It is so vast that the shell includes some well-known structures that were themselves considered as being among the largest structures of the universe: these include the Great Wall, the Hercules Superclusters, the Sloan Great Wall, the Ursa Major Supercluster, and the Corona Borealis Supercluster. At its center is found the Boötes Supercluster of galaxies, which might be associated with the initial central overdensity that generated the BAO wave. In the underdense layer between the core and the shell, there is the Boötes Void, one of the first large cosmic voids to be discovered historically.

We gave this structure a Hawaiian name, so as to honor the culture and traditions of the Hawaiian people for whom astronomy, cartography and navigation play an important role. We called it *Ho'oleilana*, inspired by a sentence of the Hawaiian Kumulipo creation chant: *Ho'oleilei ka lana a ka Po uliuli*, that can be translated as *From deep darkness came murmurs of awakening*. A fitting name for a structure born out of the sound generated in the depths of the awakening universe!

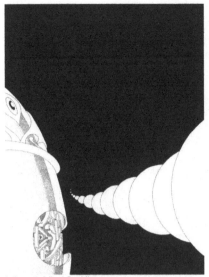

Infinity 1, Nigel Suckling

From the Contributing Editor

Galaxy Returns

Robert Silverberg

For more than a decade, beginning in 1938, John W. Campbell's *Astounding Science Fiction* dominated the science-fiction world. Campbell introduced such writers as Robert A. Heinlein, Isaac Asimov, A. E. van Vogt, L. Sprague de Camp, Theodore Sturgeon, L. Ron Hubbard, Lester del Rey and a host of others, and brought about a revolution in the writing of science fiction, steering a middle course between the serious science-oriented prose of the early magazines edited by Hugo Gernsback and T. O'Conor Sloane and the unabashed pulp style favored by newer editors like Ray Palmer and Mort Weisinger.

But in the summer of 1950 writers and readers of science fiction began to hear of the imminent arrival of an ambitious new competitor that threatened to challenge *Astounding*'s supremacy. The editor would be Horace L. Gold; his magazine would be called *Galaxy Science Fiction*, and the advance press releases promised that the new magazine would carry science fiction forward into a new golden age, making it the shaping force of the new decade of science fiction as *Astounding* had been for the last one.

Gold, fiercely opinionated and furiously intelligent, had written science fiction professionally since his teens, publishing stories even before Campbell's ascent to the editorial chair, and had worked as associate editor for a pulp-magazine chain just before the war. He wrote outstanding stories for Campbell in those years too; but then he went off to service, and when he returned it was with serious war-related psychological disabilities from which he was years in recovering.

By 1950, though, Gold was vigorous enough to want to make a head-on attack on Campbell's editorial dominance: to edit a magazine that would emulate the older editor's visionary futuristic range while at the same time allowing its writers a deeper level of psychological insight than Campbell seemed comfortable with. His intention was to liberate Campbell's best writers from what was now widely felt to be a set of constrictive editorial policies, and to bring in the best of the new writers as well; and to this end he offered his writers a notably higher rate of pay than *Astounding* had been giving them.

The first issue of *Galaxy*, resplendent in a gleaming cover printed on heavy coated stock, was dated October 1950. Its contents page featured five of Campbell's star authors—Clifford D. Simak, Isaac Asimov,

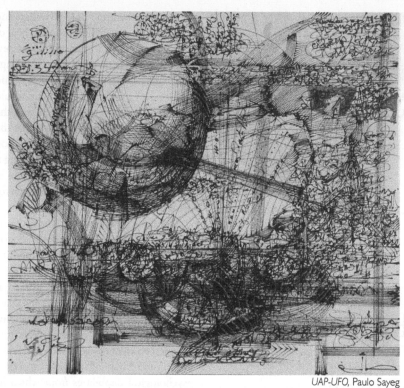

UAP-UFO, Paulo Sayeg

Fritz Leiber, Theodore Sturgeon, Frederic Brown—along with already celebrated newcomers Richard Matheson and Katherine MacLean. Issue 2 added Damon Knight and Anthony Boucher to the roster; the third, another recent Campbell star, James H. Schmitz. A new Asimov novel was serialized beginning in issue 4; the fifth had a long story by Ray Bradbury, "The Fireman," which would later become the nucleus of his novel *Fahrenheit 451*. So it went all year, and for some years thereafter. The pre-publication hype turned out to be justified: the level of performance of the new magazine was astonishingly high. Every few months *Galaxy* brought its readers stories and novels destined for classic status: Alfred Bester's *The Demolished Man*, Pohl and Kornbluth's *The Space Merchants* (called "Gravy Planet" in the magazine), Heinlein's *The Puppet Masters*, James Blish's "Surface Tension," Wyman Guin's "Beyond Bedlam," and dozens more. Though the obstreperous Gold was a difficult, well-nigh impossibly demanding editor to work with, he and his magazine generated so much excitement in the first half of the '50s that any writer who thought at all of writing science fiction wanted to write for the dazzling newcomer.

It was an exciting magazine, and it turned the field upside down practically overnight. I was delighted to begin writing for it myself beginning in 1956, and to remain a regular contributor for the next twenty years, and I am happy to find, now, that after languishing in limbo for several decades, there is once again a magazine called *Galaxy*, which summons up for me glowing memories of those great days seventy years ago when every shiny new issue brought stories never to be forgotten.

PRAXIS

David Gerrold

ONE

It wasn't a riot. It was a celebration. Our team won. They won the big one. It was important. It was the first time in living memory that the team came home with the flags, the trophies, the rings. So of course we hit the streets.

It's traditional to celebrate. Get drunk. Smoke dope. But this was special beyond special. It was time to get fucked up and go wild. Break a few windows, start some fires, flip a couple police cars. That's not a riot. That's a party. We earned it. We deserved it. We're the champions. Boo-yah!

In the morning, the lawyers explained it to me. There were two of them. They wore shiny suits and hard expressions. The law didn't see it the same way I did. According to the law, it was a riot and I'm a bad person.

So they gave me a choice. The same choice they give everyone. Pay a large fine. Very large. Or else join the Labor Corps. Three to five years, depending on the assignment. That's not really much of a choice, but it isn't supposed to be. The law sets the fine by your projected income (and in my case, that's somewhere on the south side of nothing) but even if you have an income, the fine is always going to be more than you can afford. The judge has no incentive to make it easy on you. Not while the state can show a profit on your conviction.

The Labor Corps is supposed to be a way to repay your debt to society, but it's really a for-profit arrangement. The Labor Corps buys criminal indentures from the state. That makes it government-sanctioned slavery.

I'm not stupid; slavery is about economics. If labor is cheap enough, you can build pyramids. The Labor Corps builds pyramids—or anything else anyone has the money to pay for. There was a lot of talk about it in the lockup. There's nothing else to do in there but talk. Or sleep. Or masturbate. Alone or with a friend.

The courts are backed up like a cheap toilet, so they arraign prisoners on a first-come, first-served schedule. If it's a party weekend, you can be in lockup till Wednesday or Thursday.

Somewhere in there, you get ten minutes with the lawyers. They're not there to defend you. They're there to explain why you're going to the Labor Corps. You have no choice, they say, make it easy on yourself, plead no-contest and you'll get three years instead of seven. As soon as you realize you have no choice, you agree and they send you back to lockup to wait for sentencing.

In lockup you hear the rest of it. There are no three-year or seven-year sentences. The Labor Corps pays your fine and owns your indenture. They put you to work, whatever you can do—they don't mistreat you, but they do bill you for your bed and your laundry and your meals. They bill you for cigarettes and candy bars and jumpsuits and shoes and underwear and sick calls. So it works out that you never quite pay off your bill. The Labor Corps isn't an indenture, it's a lifetime career.

Except maybe not.

There was a big Black guy sitting against the wall, looking hard and skeptical. I didn't know what he was in lockup for, but he had a wristband like the rest of us, blinking red and flashing text and numbers. His name was Mickey, but everybody called him Big Mick.

Big Mick was saying to someone, "Nah. Don't have to indenture. Request emigration."

"To where?"

"Anywhere. Go through a portal."

"A portal? Yeah, right. The other side of nowhere."

"Portals buy indentures, thirty cents on the dollar. Cheapest way out. You go, you only pay back the thirty."

"To where? Nordhel? Heavy-gee ice-world? Chip blocks off glaciers so Midwest farmers can water their beans? Then we get to buy the beans? Or maybe ammonia mining on some nameless rock—live inna tunnel where everything smells like piss? Work inna pressure suit, eat soylent and shit green? Uh-uh." That was a big guy, covered with a red tiger-tat, outlining the left half of his face. "Rather be digging new Sahara canal. Not hafta pay for my own oxy."

Big Mick shrugged. "Your choice, gospodin. Some people want other."

"Yeah? Name six."

"Just one. Praxis."

"Never heard."

"Private-financed. Six dry holes, lucky on the seventh. Yellow star. Point nine gee. Oxygen-rich. Post-Jurassic. Can't get better."

"It so good, whyn't you go?"

"Not taking everybody. Need specific skills. But I'm apped and good to go. Just waiting. Two-three days, I'm outa."

"Yeah? Maybe. What they need?"

"Carpenters, plumbers, electricians, engineers, geologists, farmers, dishwashers, trashmen—anybody who wanna work. Building a colony from ground up."

Tiger-tat wasn't impressed. "Issa catch. Always a catch."

Mick said, "Maybe. But still sound good to me. Planet has loopyh orbit. Go from inner rim of Goldilocks zone to outer edge, maybe past, but life survive. When hot, is too hot. When cold, is too cold. But not impossible. Least that what they say. It have one big continent, one big ocean. Lotsa islands. Thirty-six axial tilt—so hot at equator it have scorch belt across middle of continent. Uninhabitable. But north and south, issa useful climate. Poles are temperate, some good ice, but not enough meltwater for whole continent, so large areas of scrub and desert. Not paradise, but possibilities."

"But it has shirtsleeve zones, right?" asked a smaller man.

"Two," said Big Mick. "North and south. But two very different ecologies because of separation. Some big animals. Watch where you step, you be okay."

"Not sound too bad," said the smaller man.

"No listen anymore," snapped Tiger-tat. "Dissa recruiter!" He jabbed a finger at Big Mick. "You think we stupid? How much a bounty you get for us?"

Big Mick didn't blink. "If you no wanna go, don't go. Nobody hold gun to your head."

"Bullpiss. Not even good enough to be shit. No recruiter inna jail unless portal open onna bad place. Fukka dis." Tiger-tat shook his head and crossed to the bench on the opposite wall. Two men got out of his way and he parked himself there, folding his arms and glowering defiance.

A gospodin with shaved head, no tats, stepped up next. "What else? What you not saying?"

Big Mick smiled. "No women."

Shaved-Head frowned. "No women?"

Mick nodded. "Just robos."

"Why so?"

"Population control. Stability. They say."

Shaved-Head snorted and walked away. So did several others. But a few remained and continued questioning. I sat on the corner nearby, not facing, but I could hear the conversations clearly. I kept my eyes shut and pretended to doze. Safest way to wait.

Big Mick explained what would happen at arraignment. The judge would have your plea deal in front of him, but for the record he still had to ask, "Will you pay your fine or will you accept service in the Labor Corps?" At that point, you had the right to say, "Your Honor, I request the opportunity to apply for labor emigration. I request Praxis." (Or any other portal.)

The judge would then forward your resume, your work experience, and your rap sheet, to the requested Portal Authority. Or, if you had no planet in mind, you would be put up for bid. Some portals had representatives in court who could make an immediate decision on your application. After that, any other portal agent had ten days to put in a bid. If there were no bids, you went to the Labor Corps.

If Praxis had gone to the trouble of putting a recruiter in the lockup, they would probably have a representative in court. I listened to the whole discussion. I didn't know if Big Mick was a recruiter, but he did make a good case.

The suits had made it clear that I was going away. The videos of the riot showed me stark naked, standing on the roof of a police car, drinking beer and urinating on it. Despite the animal mask I was wearing, the barcode tattoo on my butt still gave me away. That and my federal microchip.

I knew a little bit about the portals. It was hard not to. Living in a stinkhole, you dream of escape, and the portals looked like magical doorways, so there were a lot of stories floating around about what was really out there. Supposedly the best worlds were saved for the rich, where secret pleasure domes dotted paradise landscapes, but all the rest were hellish worlds where monsters and demons sucked away your soul. Zombie-rumors staggered round the webs, refusing to die, no matter how much snopery was applied.

The truth about the portals was probably much more mundane.

Opening a hole in space is tricky. First you get a bunch of scientists and engineers to design a set of probability matrices, you use these matrices to shape a hyperstate whorl, you wait until it stabilizes, and then you stick a probe through to see what you had. Of course, you put the whole thing inside a massive, pressured dome, just in case—because nine times out of ten, you get a dry hole. A wall of rock. Empty space. Crushing gravity. A gas giant. Even de Sitter space, whatever that is. Once even, the interior of a star—that blew a hole in Montana bigger than the Barringer meteor crater. That's why portals are now staged offworld. You have to go through a staging world, sometimes two or three, to get to the portal that opens to your final destination.

Most of the portal worlds—when you do get one that's useful—are barren, but they're still good for mining gas and minerals and sometimes even ice. Frozen water is best, you can ship it or pipe it and there are no shortages of buyers, clean water is the most essential component of survival. A lot of gases are valuable, especially ammonia and nitrogen, because you can make fertilizer with them. Rare earths of all kinds, of course—sulfur, nickel, molybdenum, tin, all the metals. It's easier to carve up a barren world where there aren't any greenies to protest, so lots of big corporations have funded portal development. Cheap and easy resources were a magnet for poor nations too. It should have been a gold rush.

Only it wasn't. Because every useful portal had its own set of impossible challenges. The initial investment to develop a self-sufficient colony could be prohibitive. Every new world required its own specific sets of equipment and life-support modules.

But shirtsleeve worlds were always one-way tickets.

If there was liquid water, life was inevitable. If you opened a portal and you found oxygen in the atmosphere, it was both good news and bad. Oxygen meant there were plants producing it. And if there were plants and oxygen, then there were creatures breathing that oxygen and feeding on those plants and excreting waste for the plants to feed on. And if there were things that ate the plants, then there were very likely a lot of other things that preyed on those things that ate the plants. Where life was possible, it was inevitable—in a large messy web of complex interrelationships. A taxonomist's wet dream. A colonist's nightmare.

Because that's what Big Mick wasn't saying. A shirtsleeve world existed in a self-imposed quarantine. You could go, to me."

but you couldn't come back. Ever.

No Portal Authority was going to take the risk that something might come back to infect the homeworld. Anything shipped in from a barren world could be certified as clean—but a world with its own ecology, even a simple and primitive ecology, could still contain deadly biological time-bombs. Quarantine was the easiest solution.

And that was why Praxis needed to recruit so aggressively. It was a door of no return. If you emigrated, you could have a long life or a short life, there was no guarantee—but either way, you were going to die there.

I suppose there might be men who would want to go to Praxis for the adventure of opening up a new world, designing and building a new society. But for most, choosing Praxis would be an option only if the alternative was even more unpleasant.

And so far, I hadn't heard many good things about the Labor Corps—

TWO

"Jamie, que pasa—?"

I opened my eyes. A dark-eyed boy in a T-shirt stood in front of me. He was my age. Part of the crowd from the university. We'd all stormed out of the dorm together. José something. We'd shared a class or two.

He grinned. "I saw. You pissed on the cops."

"It seemed like a good idea at the time. What did you do?"

A rueful smile. "I threw a bottle."

"And they arrested you for that?"

"It was full of gasoline."

"You came prepared?"

"It wasn't mine. Somebody handed it

"You think the judge will believe that?"

"I know he won't."

"You're entitled to reasonable doubt."

"That doesn't exist anymore. Not where there's video."

He sat down on the bench next to me. "They swept up all of us." He waved his hand to indicate the rest of the building. "This place is filled."

"Yeah."

"You know, we're screwed."

"That thought had occurred to me."

"You got family?"

"No."

"Me neither."

"Insurance?"

"Not for this. Canceled after the Homecoming riot."

"Yeah. Me too."

He sniffed. Allergy or crying, I couldn't tell. He wiped his nose. "What are you going to do?"

"I dunno."

"I think I'm gonna option. I think Praxis."

"You been listening to Big Mick."

"Yeah." Then he added, "But Praxis has open sky. Stars. I want to see stars. Real stars. *Estrellas!*"

"But they won't be our stars. It won't even be our galaxy. It won't be anyplace anybody can recognize."

That was the thing about portals. The skies were always different. So different, they couldn't be identified. Even the lighthouse quasars were different. Nobody knew where—or even when—those other worlds existed. Something called Heisenberg uncertainty in the design matrices. You can design for one thing, but not the other. It's still mostly a guessing game. That's why you can open a portal to an unknown world that might be on the other side of the universe and a billion years from now, but you can't open a doorway to today's moon or Mars. Not yet, anyway. Maybe someday. If they ever figure out how to design the equations out to the ultimate decimal of pi.

José shrugged. "I don't care. I just want out." He looked around at the bare stone walls of the lockup. "Out of here. Out of this city. Out of this whole crappy system."

I grunted. A grunt is the safest answer. It says you heard. It doesn't say you agree. Even better, it doesn't say you disagree. Disagreement is dangerous. You can get hurt disagreeing.

"You know what I heard?" I didn't answer. He went on anyway. "I heard the reason they need so many guys on Praxis, they keep losing 'em. Yeah, maybe there are things out in the scrub that eat people, but what I heard is that the climate is so easy, you can just walk off the plantation. Go off on your own, live on the beach, eat coconuts and fish, nobody to hassle you. I heard there's a lot of guys doing that. Work just long enough to learn how things work, then take off on their own."

That was interesting. "Why don't they drag them back?" I held up my wrist to show the band. "Aren't they chipped?"

José shrugged. "Maybe it's not cost-effective to go after 'em. Maybe it's just easier to bring in new. Maybe the guys who wanna leave, you use 'em for scouting and exploring or just write 'em off as a loss. I dunno. There's gotta be something. But that's what I heard. Nobody's coming back anyway, so it's all just stories. But what if it's true? A place beyond the walls? That would be real freedom, wouldn't it?"

"I'm not sure anyone knows what freedom is anymore," I said. Having finally said it aloud, the words startled me. What did I mean by that? What did anyone mean?

José fell silent. And I was left thinking about freedom. I couldn't define it, not in words, but I didn't feel free. I didn't think anybody did anymore.

My situation—before my arrest—was a good example. I had an extended education contract. As a university-sponsored consumer, I was eligible for a federal subsidy. In return for Basic Living Expenses, the subsidy required me to take seven units per term, participate in an additional two units of research or data mining, and maintain a 2.85 or better GPA. Was that "freedom to learn"—or was it "assigned labor?" Or—as some cynics like to argue, the mandatory creation of more skilled workers for the Labor Corps.

It wasn't like I had a lot of other options. There weren't any. If you don't have options, you don't have choices—and if you don't have choices, are you really free?

That didn't matter now. Unless I was miraculously acquitted—highly unlikely, not with the video evidence—my subsidy would be canceled. Automatically null and void, under the no-strikes rule. So the only choice left was which slave camp I wanted to be sent to.

Freedom? Hah.

Compared to all that, going out into the scrub didn't seem like such a bad idea.

On the other hand—leaving Earth? Never coming back?

But then again, what had Earth done for me? It was crowded, polluted, and desperate. There wasn't any place for me here—and even if there were a place, there would be ten thousand applicants already in line ahead of me.

The argument went back and forth in my head. Yes, no, yes, no, yes, no. Unlike everything else in my experience, I couldn't detach myself from this decision, because whatever I decided, it was going to be permanent. This was a lot more life-changing than choosing between First Aid 101 and Advanced Plumbing.

After a while, I tuned out most of the noise around me. It's a necessary skill for city-dwellers, being able to withdraw inside yourself. You have no personal space beyond your skin, but you have infinite space inside your head. And if you're any good at using that space, you can explore the possibilities of actual wisdom—at least, that's what I'd learned in Basic Meditation Techniques.

One of the techniques was a very old one. Ask questions. Keep asking questions. Where does it hurt? Why does it hurt? Was there a similar hurt before this? Imagine it's a knot on a string. Pull the string up and find the earlier knot. Now keep pulling and find the earlier knot. Pull some more and find the earlier knot. Keep pulling it up until you reach the bottom-most knot.

What came up was the view from the top of the diving tower. It was too high and I was too small. I could jump off or I could climb back down. I knew I could climb back down, I'd done it before. But I didn't know if I could jump off, I'd never done that. It was an old memory. I must have been six or seven.

And as I looked at it, I realized—what I was afraid of was leaping into the unknown. I knew what life would be like in the Labor Corps. Most assignments had that same stink of ruthless regimentation. I did not know who or what I would be on Praxis. But Praxis was permanent.

José said guys went off into the scrub, lived off the land—but were they doing that because the land was so attractive?

Or were they running away from something so horrible that living off the scrub was the only desperate alternative?

The arguments about emigrating were still going on—all around me. Most of them were pretty shallow. That was to be expected. Most of these guys weren't very good at research. I was. That was the skill you most needed to succeed as an education-consumer.

José was talking again. I opened my eyes and looked at him. "Say what?"

"I know you're thinking about it. Buddy up with me. They give priority to contract families, bonded pairs, married couples, partners, even buddies—stability units they call them."

"So what?"

"They're not going to take everybody, only a few of us. If we're buddies, that ups our chances."

"I never said I wanted to go."

"But you've been thinking about it."

"I think about a lot of things. That doesn't mean I want to do them."

"You want to stay here? Be a Labor Corps slave? You do know the life expectancy of a slave, don't you? At least, on Praxis, we'd have a chance. And you have useful skills. That makes you a priority candidate. Together, we—"

I glared at him.

"I looked you up. So what? I want to get out of here. If not you—" He shrugged. He glanced around the room. "I can probably find somebody else, but you're my best shot."

"What's in it for me?"

"The difference between possibly and certainly."

Something about the way he said it. It was a good answer.

I stopped myself from replying and just looked at him. Small, wiry, clear-eyed.

Mixed descent, hard to say, certainly Asian, possibly some African-American, a smidge of Caucasian, and definitely Latino. He had a California accent. That would explain a lot. But I wasn't going to hold that against him. Definitely a contract student like me. And probably very smart. He had that look—focused. And he was precise in his language. That was usually a giveaway.

And he was studying me too. "James, haven't you been paying any attention to the news? The regressives have made the universities an issue. They're whining that it's gotten too expensive to subsidize the education contracts."

"They can't cancel the contracts. That's illegal. It's a federal guarantee. Paying people to get educated is good business. And it's good for the national economy. And even if they could, that'd just create a whole new class of unemployed, homeless, and hungry. And angry. And educated enough to make waves. We know how to vote. They can't be that stupid."

"Yeah, I took that same class. Remember?"

"So what's your point?"

"They're not going to cancel the contracts. They're just going to cancel the contract holders. Us. That's what this is about. Haven't you been following the news?"

"Which news? Which set of lies and misinformation?"

He ignored the question. He spoke very seriously now. "The Labor Corps needs thirty thousand conscripts a month. Every time they take on a new job—like the Sahara canals or whatever—that number goes up another five to ten thousand. Those bodies have to come from somewhere." He pointed around. "This is it, James. We're being purged."

"Interesting theory." But it kinda made sense.

"It's not a theory. The cops knew there was going to be a riot, they even planned it. Think about it. All those tanks, all those cops, all that riot gear, all those buses lined up. They had to be prepping for weeks. That stuff doesn't happen by accident. It was planned. The cops swept up over a thousand of us in one night. They're still sweeping. Do you know what that's worth to the city in indenture contracts? A couple hundred million— at least that much after all the bribes and payoffs. No, there aren't going to be any acquittals. Unless you have a family that can outbid the Labor Corps, you're on your way to Africa."

I didn't answer. Conspiracy theories were cheap. I'd heard a lot of them. Some of them even made sense. This one did. But that didn't prove anything either. But whether or not José was right, the outcome was the same.

"Say yes. We gotta do this. Really."

"I don't gotta anything. I don't even know you."

"My name is José Miguel Rodríguez-Chan. I am twenty-three years old. Ortho-male. Heterosexual. Unmarried. No children. I had a girlfriend for four months, but she took a job in Texas as a surrogate-programmer. I have comp-leted majors in biology, agriculture, mechanical engineering, journalism and music. I have no brothers or sisters, my father is dead, my mother lives in Buenos Aires and doesn't speak to me because I didn't return to Argentina with her. I should have. What else do you need to know?"

"Why me?"

"Because we're both here. And we know each other. Do you want to go with a stranger?" He added, "Okay, we don't

know each other all that well, but we get along well enough. We usually vote the same way at dorm-bloc meetings. And we were in the same class on Self-Sufficiency, Planning and Preparation. I sat three rows behind you. You were the smartest one in the room. Well, almost. I beat your scores a couple times. When I looked you up, I ran our psychometrics. We're compatible—seventy-eight percent. If we had time, we'd be good friends. But we don't have time. We have to decide now—before sentencing."

I took a deep breath. He was almost convincing.

But before I could say anything, the buzzer went off, the lights came up, and they were herding us into the courtroom, all fifty of us.

THREE

Judge Villanova looked tired and unhappy. She'd been hearing cases all day. She'd probably heard every possible story by now. We entered the court and each of us in turn held our wristbands over the security scanner. She didn't even look at us. She sat on her high bench, watching our case files roll up on her display, a sour expression on her face.

The first few cases were up-and-down. The accused stepped forward, pled guilty, and accepted a voluntary indenture to the Labor Corps. "Let it be entered." Bang. "Next?"

Then she called Shaved-Head. He stepped up to the dock and said, "I request emigration for myself and my contract-family."

She didn't look surprised. "Is your family here?"

"Yes, Your Honor." He pointed.

"Have them step up."

Tiger-Tat and one other man joined

Shaved-Head in the dock. Judge Villanova had them identify themselves. She checked off their names on her display. "Are you all three agreed on the terms of your contract?" They nodded yes. "And your choice of portal?"

"Praxis, Your Honor."

"Very well." She made a note. "Is the agent for Praxis in court?"

A broad-shouldered man on the side stood up. "Here." He wore a glistening suit and data-glasses.

"These three are remanded to your custody. You have twenty-four hours to take them or throw them back. Next case," She banged her gavel. "No talking, please."

She worked her way through several more prisoners. Then: "José Miguel Rodríguez-Chan?"

José stepped to the dock. He put his hand on the scan-panel to confirm his identity. Judge Villanova looked at her display, looked at him, shook her head, and said, "I really hate sentencing contract students. You had a good thing going—"

"Your Honor?" José spoke up. "I request labor emigration. For myself and my partner."

She looked down at him. "Who's your partner?"

José turned and pointed at me. "James Patrick Dolan."

"Step up to the dock. Put your hand on the panel."

I started to protest, but realized that she wouldn't hear my protest until I identified myself. I went and stood next to José. I put my right hand on the scan-panel. It blinked green.

"James Patrick Dolan, are you in a partnership with José Miguel Rodríguez-Chan?"

"Um—" José grabbed my hand quickly and squeezed it. The Judge looked over the top of her glasses, saw us holding hands, and made a note on the display in front of her. She looked back down at me. "I need to hear you say it aloud."

José squeezed my hand harder.

And I squeezed back.

"Yes'm," I said. Then louder, "Yes, Your Honor."

"Thank you." She frowned at her display. "I don't see a record of it here. When was this partnership confirmed? How long have you been together?"

"Six months," José said quickly. "We're in the same dorm-bloc and we were in the same class six months ago. We just haven't—It should be in your records there. Self-Sufficiency?"

"I see." She frowned. She took her glasses off, rubbed the bridge of her nose with her eyes closed, put her glasses back on, and sighed. "If this is a contract of convenience, boys—"

"No, ma'am. It's not. We're real."

"—because I see a lot of these last-minute partnerships. Attempts to avoid the Labor Corps. But I'm willing to give you the benefit of the doubt." She looked to me. "You want to go to Praxis too?"

"Uh—yes, Your Honor, I do."

She wasn't convinced. "Is that a yes-it's-a-good-idea yes? Or is that a whatever-it-takes-no-matter-what commitment?"

"Um." I looked to José. His eyes were bright. I looked back to the judge. "It's a commitment," I said. It was what she wanted to hear. José squeezed my hand tight.

"All right. Well, let's test it. Mr. Firestone?"

The agent from Praxis stood up. "Yes, Your Honor?" He took off his data-glasses.

"You have the files of these two in front of you?"

"Yes, Your Honor."

"How do they look?"

"Not bad, I'd really prefer to interview them before accepting their indentures, but—"

"If they were married, would that improve their prospects?"

"Of course, but—"

"On a scale of 1 to 10?"

"If there are no disqualifying conditions." He glanced at the tablet in his hand. "I don't see any here. We would accept them."

"Thank you." Judge Villanova turned back to us, an unspoken question on her face.

"Uh—"

José squeezed my hand again. Harder than ever. I pulled away reflexively.

"Mr. Dolan?"

"I—uh. Yeah. Um. I just hadn't realized—" I swallowed hard and tried again. "Whatever it takes, Your Honor. No matter what." I took José's hand again.

"Mr. Dolan, Mr. Rodríguez-Chan, I have the authority to marry you. Right now, in this court. Is that your request?"

We looked at each other, nervously. She was testing us. This was not what either of us had expected. But José faced her and nodded. "Yes, Your Honor." He squeezed my hand.

I took a deep breath and agreed. "Yes. It is. Yes."

"Mm. I still don't believe you. But I'm required by law to honor your request for emigration. And I'm required by law to recognize and affirm your partnership contract. If that's what you really want. Last chance to back out…?"

I didn't say anything; neither did José.

"All right." She looked from José to me. "Are you both single consenting adults? Are you entering into this contract of your own free will? Are you free of any

and all previous legal obligations and encumbrances? Place your right hands on the panels in front of you—thank you."

She looked at her own display. "José Miguel Rodríguez-Chan, do you take James Patrick Dolan to be your lawful wedded husband, with all of the attendant privileges, rights, benefits, and responsibilities of the marriage contract, for—" She stopped. "Duration?"

"Unlimited," said José.

"You're sure?"

"Sí."

"Mr. Dolan? Is that your understanding as well?"

"Uh-huh, yes."

She turned back to José. "—for as long as you both shall choose, in a partnership indivisible except by mutual consent? Mr. Rodríguez-Chan?"

"Sí, Señora. I do," José said.

She focused on me and repeated the same question. "James Patrick Dolan, do you take José Miguel Rodríguez-Chan to be your lawful wedded husband, with all of the attendant privileges, rights, benefits, and responsibilities of the marriage contract for as long as you both shall choose, in a partnership indivisible except by mutual consent? Mr. Dolan?"

I nodded, swallowed hard, realized I was abruptly feeling something very strange. I managed to croak, "Yes, I do."

"You do understand, both of you, that marriage is a partnership. It's not about what you're going to get out of it. It's about what you're going to put into it. I want you to look at each other, right now. Take each other's hands—"

We did. José's eyes were wide.

"Are you committed to contributing to this person opposite you? No, don't say it to me. Say it to him."

José thought for a second, then he said, "James Patrick, you make a difference to me. I promise to make the same difference to you."

My throat was suddenly dry. My voice cracked. "José Miguel. You—you found me. You saved me. So my life is yours."

"I've heard worse." Judge Villanova said, "Do you have rings?"

"No, Your Honor."

"Bailiff? Do we have—"

"Yes, Judge." The bailiff held up a small cardboard box. She was a big Black woman. She had pulled the rings out of her desk before the first "I do."

"Nothing fancy," said Judge Villanova. "But consider this a gift of the court."

José opened the box. Two plain black rings. "José Miguel, repeat after me. 'James Patrick Dolan, with this ring, I thee wed—'"

He slid the ring on my finger. It felt cold and strange.

"James Patrick?"

"José Miguel Rodríguez-Chan, with this ring, I thee wed—" I put the ring on his finger. He held his left palm to mine. The rings beeped and glowed for an instant. They were activated. I'd always know how near or far he was.

We turned back to Judge Villanova.

"Your marriage is now recorded and certified by the Commonwealth. You may kiss your husband."

"Uh—" I turned to José.

"Shut up," he said. He held my face between his hands and pulled me down to him. A quick peck on the lips. Then a second kiss, this one a little longer. I'd been kissed by friends before, the occasional friendship kiss, it didn't bother me, but this wasn't a friendship kiss. It was just ... different.

He let me go and Judge Villanova said, "Congratulations." The bailiff, the court clerk, and Mr. Firestone echoed her. Others in the courtroom applauded.

The clerk reached under her desk and pulled out two copies of the marriage certificate, still warm from the printer. "Mazel tov." Two seconds later, "And here are your indenture documents."

"Good luck on your emigration interview," Judge Villanova said. "Don't get thrown back. Going to the Labor Corps—that would automatically annul your marriage." Then she added, "Prove me wrong. I don't want to see you in my court again."

"Uh, yes. Thank you, ma'am. Your Honor."

"We'll see." She looked past my shoulder. "Next?"

The bailiff pointed us toward an interview room. José took me by the hand and led me out, "Come on, husband."

We hope that you have enjoyed this excerpt. Please stay tuned for the release of the full novella coming soon.

Solemnicus, Bruce Pennington

Starship Sloane Publishing

—COMING SOON—

A NOVELLA BY DAVID GERROLD

PRAXIS

WITH A FOREWORD BY JOHN SHIRLEY

A wonderfully realized and self-contained story about sexual ambivalence (amongst many other things) that nevertheless leaves you hoping Gerrold's next SF tale picks up where this one leaves off.

—Nigel Suckling

Master of the imagination David Gerrold does it again, Praxis is a story of letting go, communication, and acceptance. For men to find a new way they must first redefine manhood, break from an oppressive society, and together learn what it means to become a new type of human.

—Jean-Paul L. Garnier

Praxis is one of the very few books I've read where the premise of the society/world/universe is so interesting that it engages regardless of the plot. And the plot is a novel and unusual possible human situation, driven by the constraints of what may well come to pass, where traditional space-opera is dragged screaming and kicking into a future with brand-new conventions. What Praxis is really (as is all the best SF), is the intro for an never-ending epic. But the evocative set-up is what I look for in speculative literature—and this book serves as a magnificent springboard for the reader's imagination.

—F. J. Bergmann

The thought-provoking story of two partners set to embark on a one-way trip to a planet that's all men—a literary exploration of human relationships in a brutal society seeking to colonize the universe.

—Dr. Daniel Pomarède

COVER ART BY BOB EGGLETON
STARSHIP SLOANE PUBLISHING

Texting from Forty Light Years Away

Whether this reaches the other end of the ansible,
I'll never know. I can't afford video or even audio

right now—and couldn't bear to see you, anyway,
or hear your voice. Once, I shamelessly spent

all I had on making myself whatever you wanted;
I bought whatever glittered onscreen, watched

my simulacra pixellate and blur in webshops,
wore vices and vivisectioned visions, bargained

across xenolinguistic barriers, at ruinous rates
of exchange. My ignorance of you didn't matter;

I constructed the lover I wanted out of whole,
sequined cloth. I saw my reflection fragmented

in the faceted lenses you wore instead of eyes.
Estranged from my former friends, that vertigo

kept me from loneliness. I followed you from
city to city, planet to planet, currency flowing

like methane rivers beneath constructs that linked,
like bridges, the beautiful universes. I think

you enjoyed leading me on, asking me for small
sacrifices, then big ones: role-playing, gender

manipulations, implants—the endless surgeries.
The only way I could tell what I had become

was by watching the gray faces of other humans
distance themselves. Soon your eyes too lost focus

whenever they saw me in my myopic reverence,
darted elsewhere, quickly, like swooping birds.

I'd had delicious dreams instead of a relationship;
pickpocket of hearts, you'd had the latest in a series

of diversions. To balance things between us, I pined
and shouted alternately; I gathered each red wound

into a lopsided bouquet. Only, you spoke all the alien-
tainted tongues. Except you could just disappear.

I catch a glimpse of myself in the extruded curve
of a viewport and am no less strange than if it were

a perfectly flat mirror. Although none of their letters
are from human languages, signs are everywhere.

—*F. J. Bergmann*

Namata, Paulo Sayeg

You Recognized Her
Zdravka Evtimova

Leisure was approaching. You recognized it in your bones, the tourists said. They added that you knew it was there because you could not sleep at night. There was that pleasant itching in your skin. Number 111 was an odd, but nondescript, little planet. People soon became accustomed to the strange mountains that rose and fell apart under their feet during Leisure. Leisure ended and the shuddering hills vanished. The mountain chains turned into flat and dull plains, which slept serenely until the next Leisure. Then the land swelled without warning, hills jumped out of the blue, mounds jutted out, wriggled and writhed before they all evaporated without a trace. The squirming hills made no difference to the tourists.

The precious thing about Number 111 was Leisure. You observed no laws— you simply did whatever you pleased, the tourists bragged. You could slit anybody's throat. Blood made no difference, they knew, for during Leisure no one could die. Tourists admitted that they felt pain, yes, but neither they nor the targets they chose met their maker. Death was virtually non-existent because guys like me collected the mutilated bodies and took them to Perna.

Perna was the plateau that regenerated ripped intestines, slashed chests, and torn viscera. Leisure made you kill and kiss, the wealthy tourists told me. Nothing compared to that bliss. You just had to catch the fragrance of Leisure. That was easy to do. Leisure didn't make me feel its fragrance. It only made me hate the Perna plateau.

I didn't want to be a body collector anymore, but there was big money in it.

There was a jar on my cupboard I looked at day and night. That jar made me feel crazy. There is hope, I said to myself. There is still hope she might be back. There's still hope. That was why I didn't leave the damn planet.

Nadya.

It was the tag sewn to the collar of her shirt that made it clear she was one of the regulars. "Nadya" her tag said. It had three blue notches on it, and that meant she'd been at the holidaymakers' beck and call three consecutive Leisure spells. That was an awful lot.

She was pretty, of course. All the regulars were. Women, children, men, all were very attractive. I'd been working as a body collector on Perna for years, and not a single body of a regular target was plain. The plateau rejected dirty bodies, squashed chests or disfigured faces, but it readily took bodies without fingers, hands, or eyes.

I was greedy. They paid well for perfectly clean bodies that were in good shape. They took them from you, checked them, then put the bodies on the flat ground. "They" were the machines the guys from Earth had installed five Leisure spells ago.

The Perna plateau was peaceful all the time. No hills sprouted from it at times of Leisure, and its soil didn't quake. There were no rocks there, not even sands. The plateau was smooth like ice. I guessed it was Perna that exuded the smell that killed the pain and healed the injuries. No one knew for sure. Perna simply cured you during Leisure.

"Don't touch me!" Nadya had said.

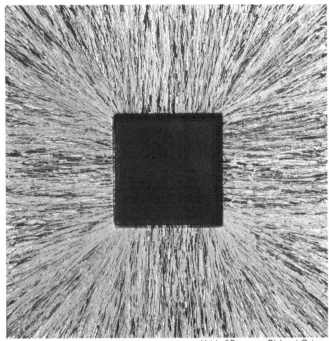

Void of Remorse, Richard Grieco

If the organs of a body were defective, you didn't get a cent for it. The Plateau didn't regenerate sick lungs or infected spleens. So I checked the organs myself and replaced the malfunctioning ones. It was worth it. I had a lot of money; unfortunately a lot was never enough. I wanted to buy a plot from the healing plateau, and I could well afford it. I was the richest body collector on Perna.

Nadya was screaming in pain when I found her. There was nothing extraordinary about that. She was one of the regulars, and they all screamed. They came to Number 111, lured by the prospect of quick money. I felt kind of sorry for them. Some rich clients had favorite regulars and booked them well in advance. Often clients and regulars got drunk together, waiting for Leisure. The regulars had contracts and everything was perfectly legal, even experimental sex. Perna cured all regular targets, and

no one died. Nothing was interesting any more.

When I saw Nadya, I froze in my tracks. I knew.

Nadya's left ear was missing. There was no bleeding, no wound, just healthy pink rims where normally an ear should be. There simply was no ear. At a certain point, I caught the thin, sweet smell of the ocean.

Few could catch the smell of the ocean on Number 111.

I could. And I knew what the smell meant.

The Insurance Agency paid me to find the bodies of the wealthy clients and take good care of them while I dragged them to the plateau. The clients paid me, too. They wanted me to have their organs inspected, because an injured organ caused wrinkles on the cheeks, hardly visible wrinkles, it was true, but rich guys hated them all the same. I made big money doing something dangerous for the big shots: they paid me most dearly to ward them off from the water.

The plateau was helpless before the ocean of Number 111. The water was transparent. It dissolved everything that fell into it: shoes, hair, bones, and bodies—no matter how rich their owners were. So the bigwigs paid me to steer them clear from the ocean. I often grabbed them before they collapsed from a mountain that squirmed under their feet; sometimes the land split, and water gushed out from the hideous crack. The bad thing was that the plateau could not regenerate any tissue that the ocean had dissolved. I tried once. I dissolved a wisp of Nadya's hair in a jug of water.

Something strange happened. When Leisure began and hills popped up, quaking and breaking as if the land were ocean, I heard somebody say, "Don't take me to the plateau."

I recognized the voice. It was Nadya's. I thought I was only dreaming or hallucinating. The voice kept on mouthing the same words—now crooning, now raving. I recorded it many times, trying to rule out the crawling suspicion that it was my imagination shouting at Leisure.

Body collectors often went crazy. Ordinary guys feared us and said we, the collectors, were freaks. We didn't feel the pleasure of Leisure. We were greedy and mercenary.

I was the greediest among them.

Yes, Nadya's voice was there, real and soft, recorded by the most expensive equipment you could buy on the market. One day I threw out the jug in which I had dissolved a wisp of her hair. My hut was cozy but inexpensive. I could never be sure when a hill would push its way up to the sky under the floor of my living room, destroying my home in a matter of seconds. The day after I threw out the jug, the steep slopes around my hut screamed at me, "Don't take me to the plateau!" The hill where I poured the water became Nadya's voice.

After a week of screaming, the hill broke, ripping open the valley, and I saw a figure in the blue distance. It was Nadya I saw. She approached me, looking beautiful, so beautiful I forgot everything else, the wiggling hills, the stalking valleys, the rich clients and their targets. Then suddenly all was quiet. Nadya was gone, the hills disappeared. Leisure had come to its end.

Ends came abruptly, without warning. They always took me by surprise. The quiet I enjoyed so much in the past was now unbearable. There were no mountains, no quaking ridges and gorges; the ocean was peaceful dead water I could swim in with some of the regulars. I got drunk with them. I often made love to the prettiest women free of charge. That was illegal, of course.

Nadya was different. She'd been collected three times before I stumbled upon her. I could smell a dying man from two miles. I could feel the moment when the mountain would crash down, interring the bodies—my only hope of getting rich. I sensed the tremor before the crests of the hills ripped the low sky. I fought the dust that suffocated the regulars and marred their bodies.

Nadya was pretty, but if you were pretty and a woman you were in store for a hard time. Wealthy clients made you a target. Their lawyers paid you a lot to keep quiet. Pretty women were desperate for money. I had seen a woman dance on a thin layer of ice over the ocean during Leisure. I worked for a client who paid me to scoop a pail of water from the ocean then he made his target dip her finger in the pail. The water dissolved the finger in a flash and remained clear, transparent, quiet. A scream rent the air; that was the target's scream, but only experienced body collectors could distinguish it amidst the roar of the rising and folding mountains. I had found eleven women's bodies without fingers.

I did my best to make the missing finger grow again; I kept the bodies for a week on the plateau. Nothing came out of that. I had made love to women who had lost their hands.

"You can't imagine the bliss during intimate contacts after that," one woman, a client, told me.

"After what?" I asked her.

"I think the target's ear I dissolved gave the water fear and excitement. My sex life improved incredibly after that."

I was an avaricious man, a very avaricious one. My client was very rich.

"What was your target's name?" I asked her out of curiosity.

"As a rule, I don't ask my targets their names," she answered. "But this time the girl was particularly good looking. Her name was Nadya."

I froze in my tracks.

"Do you think I can convince Nadya to dip her breasts into the water for me?" she asked.

I hit the woman. I hit her hard.

It was the first time in my life I'd hit a client.

I knew Nadya had only one toe on her right foot.

"Doesn't it feel awkward that way? Doesn't it hurt?" I asked her when I took her out of the plateau.

"No," she said. "I feel no pain at all."

"You gave that bitch four of your toes," I said. "You should have made a fortune by now."

"A fortune is not enough," she said.

"I want to buy Perna. I want to buy the whole planet, its Leisure periods and its nasty water." A smile crept on her lips. "Then I'll blow it up."

"You are crazy," I told her.

"I am," she whispered.

Then we made love. It had never been so beautiful with other women, maybe because I was sorry for her. Loving her was magnificent, like loving the wind. She didn't feel like a regular. She was gentle and brittle. She was lovely. I had rarely felt sorry for anybody before.

"I have a bad headache," Nadya had said. "My head throbs. Please, kiss me on the forehead."

I kissed her forehead. It was smooth like a child's. Then she fell asleep smiling.

"My headache is gone," she said when she woke up. "It's beautiful when you kiss me."

"I don't want you to go with other clients," I heard myself saying. I didn't mean to. The words escaped my lips. Thank God she didn't say anything. Imagine a toeless regular sobbing on your shoulder! I hated the thought of it. Thank God she had kept silent then.

"Why don't you want me to bring you to the plateau?" I asked. In the beginning I was just curious. I guessed she made a lot of money. The clients paid generously if you agreed to let your toes dissolve into the water.

"Have you ever been to the plateau?" she whispered.

"No," I said.

"I've been there a dozen times," she sat up, staring at the wasteland of blue sands that was as flat as the ocean.

"How does it feel on the plateau?" I asked. She said nothing for a long time.

"Kiss me on the forehead," she suddenly pleaded, trembling. "Please, kiss me. That horrible headache ..."

It was the first time in my life it had felt sweet to touch human skin. I knew skin cost a lot. I often replaced parts of my client's faces, and I chose good new skin for them. Nadya's skin was odd. I could swear there were ripped hills and flat valleys in it. There was fear and sorrow in that skin.

I could have asked her to stay with me. Back then I thought she'd make no difference. She was another vanishing hill, another body I'd take money for. I didn't know she was the only woman whose headache I could turn into peace. I didn't know I'd miss the blue valleys in her skin. I didn't know I'd missed the disappearing hill only because she had walked on it, making it her hill.

The body collectors were a tough lot. I was pretty tough, too.

Nadya asked me, "Can I stay with you? I'll clean your hut, and I'll build it again when Number 111 breaks it. I'll cook for you."

"How can you cook?" I asked her. "You can't walk quickly. You don't have enough toes on your feet. You stagger."

I hated it when someone touched my things, my expensive equipment. I was afraid she might steal something. Women were cheap. Each cost less than the tent that protected my bodies from getting dirty in the dust of the rumbling hills.

"Okay," she said. "I'll go. I hope you'll be happy with your equipment."

"We may meet during the next Leisure," I told her. "You know where you can find me. I always build my hut near the plateau."

It was so quiet, a deep transparent peace that was the most precious thing on Perna. When Leisure was over, there were no tourists and no clients, no sick people who flew to Perna hoping that Leisure would last forever. There was no death on Number 111 during Leisure.

"Kiss me on the forehead," she said. "You'll do me a favor, and it won't cost you anything."

Her skin was smooth—it tasted of the ocean and the deep quiet. The mountains had vanished, and the planet was an endless blue plain.

Nadya didn't even say good-bye. I watched her go, thinking of the red, healthy-looking rims on the spot where her ear should be. Suddenly she turned around and whispered, "I think I love you." That was a silly thing to say. Love was as cheap as the specks of dust on the infinite plain.

Another Leisure spell came and ended. I made even more money, and I could now buy a plot on the plateau. I hoped I'd meet Nadya. I wondered how she coped with her headaches. I felt like climbing the hills she had slept on. I asked my clients if they'd met a thin woman with disfigured feet, yes, three or four toes missing. She'd lost an ear, too.

"You don't tell me anything in particular," the clients answered me. "All regular female targets look like the one you've just described."

"Her name is Nadya," I said, realizing how stupid I'd been. You came to Perna to dissolve your target's fingers in the water. Her name hardly mattered at all. I had enough money, and I could hire a private eye, but that would be ludicrous. No one searched for women on Number 111.

One day a big boat stopped in front of my hut. Leisure was just over, and there were no tourists, no clients. It was the spell of deep quiet when all mountains were dead.

A woman entered. She hadn't knocked on the door. I knew that woman. That was the only client I had hit in my long career of a body collector.

"This is Nadya," she said and lifted a jar half full of transparent liquid under my nose. "I splashed the rest of her on my husband. Our sex life is glorious now."

I looked at the jar the woman was holding in her hands. It was big and round, perfectly transparent. I looked at the woman. She was small and plump, her face round and smirking. Then I suddenly knew what her face reminded me of.

It was like the flat, dead outlines of Perna, the healing plateau.

I didn't know how it happened. Maybe the hills were to blame, I was not sure. Maybe a mountain spilled some water out of the jar as it pushed its way to the clouds. Maybe in an unthinking moment I poured it out of the window, or maybe another girlfriend of mine, another regular target, spilled the water in a fit of jealousy.

When the hills started to quake and wriggle, dust rose from the beach. The dust over the hill spoke. "The headache! The headache!"

The dust was Nadya's voice.

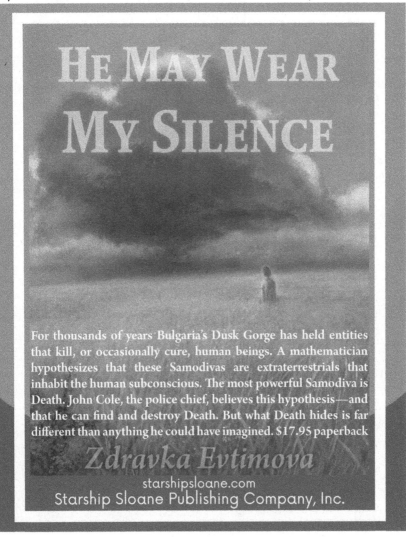

HAiRY HULLABALOO

poems by
RiCHARD STEVENSON

iLLUSTRATiONS BY
CARLA STEiN

This is a book positively brimming with wonderfully entertaining, splendidly absurd, uproariously humorous, and deeply meaningful poetry involving various cryptid creatures of lore. Insight on the human condition, social and environmental commentary, and just plain fun are on riotous display in the pages of this book. Written by the supremely skilled Canadian wordsmith Richard Stevenson and adorned with delightful illustrations by the Canadian artist Carla Stein, this vibrant book of poetry shines brightly with inspired imagination and creativity. ISBN 9798988634225. $15.95.

starshipsloane.com
Starship Sloane Publishing Company, Inc.

Dusk of the Dead

Gareth L. Powell

The dead came back. They climbed from their graves and shambled the streets. But they weren't biting anyone. There was no transmission of virus. Mostly, they just seemed to hang around bus stops and late night shop doorways. You glimpsed them from the morning train, standing beneath lamp posts or clustered on the canal towpath. They didn't need to eat or talk. They were just there, lingering instead around the trees and hedges of the neighbourhood like bonfire smoke on a still evening.

I had to push past one the other night, as I came out of the shop on the corner. He was standing on the pavement and looking up at the clouds, letting the evening's fine drizzle pool in his open mouth. As I moved to pass him, he lowered his face and I found myself confronted with cloudy, rheumy eyes in a lined, leathery face the colour of spoiled milk, and a musty smell, sweet and melancholic, like a damp overcoat left in a long-forgotten attic. Rainwater ran from his slack lips.

I didn't know what else to do, so I wished him a good evening.

I guess that may have been the first kind word he'd received since clawing his way from his mouldering coffin, because his head jerked and the eyes swivelled loosely back and forth, as if trying to focus on my face.

He wheezed like a punctured bellows. "Evening?"

"Um, yes." I'd never heard one speak before. I'm not entirely sure anyone had. "Yes, it's nearly half-past eight."

They're Always Watching Me, No. 40, Dave Vescio

"Half-past …"

"Are you all right?" It was a stupid question, but I couldn't simply turn and walk away. "Can I get you anything?" I rustled in my pocket for some coins. "A couple of quid for a cup of tea?" I pressed them into his clammy grip.

He looked down at the money without seeming to understand what it was, and then let it fall from his open hand.

"I don't need money."

I watched the coins roll on the pavement. I wanted to reach down and pick them up.

"Then what do you need?"

He pinned me with his blank, misted stare. The breeze ruffled through the damp hair wisps clinging to his scalp, and he ran a black tongue over his cracked lower lip.

"Less," he said.

35

An Interview with Bruce Pennington

Justin T. O'Conor Sloane

Sloane: Bruce, I am honored that you agreed to do this interview. Thank you!

What is the deepest source of your inspiration?

Pennington: Without any doubt the main source of inspiration for my pictures has invariably been my own imagination. Since childhood that has provided a limitless wealth of imagery experienced during the "dream state" or the "awakened state" (both often overlap during the creative process).

What key piece of advice would you give aspiring SFF artists?

During my post-art-school years, I had a fair share of rejections by publishers and ad agencies, etc., but my own sense of unique ability to create wonderful imagery kept me going; so, my advice to would-be SFF artists is "Never give up!" Self-confidence is essential. To which I must add – never produce a work of casual or cynical inferiority, however uninspiring the job might be! It could cost you in the long run.

You create magnificent SFF art using traditional tools, media, and techniques. What do you think about AI-generated art? How about generative art? In your view, do these methods produce true art, or an illusion of art? Are we removing ourselves from the natural creative process, or are these methods ultimately just an extension of that very same creative process?

The effects from computer-generated digital art can be extremely attractive and even startling at times, but they can't be equal to the traditional control of every tiny square centimeter that artists of the past were so skilled at.

Which professional accomplishment(s) are you most pleased with as an artist?

Being continuously employed by publishers from 1967 to the mid-'90s proved that I must have had something that they found attractive.

Who and what are some of your most profound artistic influences?

Without doubt some of the art and sculpture of the 19th century was awesome. That era still remains my all-time favorite! In fact, my rambling sermons against ugly modern "starkitecture" and art "at the cutting edge" of today's new emerging talents have labeled me as some kind of crank among the younger generation. But I held these opinions even when I was in my twenties at art school.

Finally, a perhaps impossible question: if you had to choose just one of your works of art as a favorite, which would it be and why?

Sorry, but I'll have to politely dodge out of that one, because my personal opinions about my own works thus far are invariably changing with the passage of time.

Cheers and thanks for your interest!

Thank you, Bruce! Here's to health and happiness!

Constant Dawn

Eliane Boey

Small Fingers shouts through my earpiece. "You got to cut her loose."

I can't lose the *Dawn*.

My lungs are crushed, and the ship of dreams slips between my fingers. Behind me, the minibulker recalculates, as the dark matter hurricane gathers its skirts around Brani Station. This salvage means a new life for Ziyi and I.

Only, it wasn't the *Constant Dawn* that needed salvaging.

※

I hadn't thought about the Stellamaris fleet until the OpenSpace alert a month ago that they'd abandoned a ship in a storm off Brani Station. Award to be posted for salvage. We were on deck of the *Tianbao*, playing a vintage board game, a present from Ziyi; Fingers talking about the time he scraped utillium fragments from a rock trawled off starboard. Before our employer, Amalgamated Extraction and Recovery, had body scans between shifts.

I said, "If I had my Ti-alloy net, we'd have hauled it back to the Claw. Get at the toy inside."

"Stellamaris's net," Fingers said.

"That company owes me. Drifting their ships in layup north of the Moon because the market 'didn't make sense'. Signing off in a recession made no sense to me, either."

"Still landed here as the highest-compensated garbage collector in space."

"Retriever-recycler," I raised an emphatic finger. "Now I'm sweeping for Amalgamated, that beauty of a net trawling scraps off the side, when I could be going after salvage awards myself."

"The *Constant Dawn*?" Fingers snorted. "Toads can look out of wells, Silver."

"What's a well?"

"Stupid kid. Anyway, this rock was so big I almost couldn't find a refiner to flip it."

"Why'd you come back, then?" I threw the dice far across the table, like they were the problem.

Small Fingers replied. "I *like* it up here."

※

When we hit the Space Labour Convention's maximum equivalent Earth months in orbit, Amalgamated sends a vessel of relief crew to the *Tianbao*, swapping us out for shore leave. Freeport, first stop after the Yokohama Wormhole, is the first co-governed international free trade station, aglow in the neon-lit endless night of its business and pleasure strip, Beach Road. Ziyi and I were sitting on the Beach, watching the artificially churned surf of electric blue chlorine cut with distilled water, thinking of the places on Earth where the sand belonged, when they said, "Think you'll get called out for the Stellamaris job?"

Ziyi monitors the cargo terminal AI on Brani Station. I was at the lobby bar of the Freeport Banyan Tree Hotel, stewing warm whisky in fresh self-loathing, when they sat beside me and ordered a boulevardier. We've shared shore leave so many times now, our work schedules have begun to sync.

"Maybe. My schedule's open."

I gave their shoulder a squeeze.

Our ship's course was set for Brani at the soonest convenient wormhole crossing. Debris clean-up job. If Ziyi knew I'd be close to their station, they'd set me up with the Port Authority for a job interview. Being closer to them is one thing, but it'll mean saying goodbye to ever landing a big salvage award. Big enough to think about setting up somewhere with Ziyi that isn't a capsule on a second-tier station.

✳

It was the last full day of our shore leave on Freeport, and I was still thinking about the *Constant Dawn*.

"You know what Stellamaris valued her at?"

Ziyi shrugged, lying on the Beach with a towel from our discount hotel.

"2.5 mil SGBit. The bastard pro-rated my wages for 'bad market' days and he's letting 2.5mil drift in the dark for another cycle."

"You saw the storm warning. No crew will go out after her until it passes." They watched as a gathering wave approached. "Maybe you'll be here longer, this time."

"Or, someone with balls could get in first. Claim the full award." I brushed sand off my arms and folded them around myself. "An award like that—without a shipowner to slurp it all and spit out scraps for bonus—could buy a few things. We might get to rent a studio on Delta with a view of this Beach."

Ziyi said, "You hold on to this job, Silver. Station-side visas are only getting harder to renew." The wave crashed.

"Amalgamated will cut me loose as soon as the contract ends. The only thing certain is my window for getting that award."

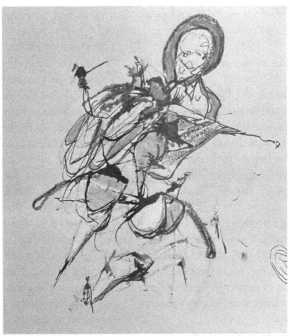

An Alien's Technology, Ronan Cahill

"How about, instead of sailing into a storm for a ship that could be anywhere, we make a real plan?" The wave pulled away.

I said, "This is as real for me as it is for you."

Ziyi turned from me, to the Embarkment. We could hear the muffled boarding and arrival announcements for passengers, and the job completion pings from cargo-handling. "The terminal's facing a labour shortage over storm season. I'm expected to renew."

"More storms mean more salvage work."

"You're addicted to storm-chasing. You haven't thought about the station-side port jobs I sent."

I spoke through my teeth. "I'm doing this for us. Look at me and tell me I'm qualified to be more than a garbage collector."

Ziyi got up off the towel.

I called after them, "You said you liked it up here!"

✳

When the storm met us as we pulled into expected casting range of the *Constant Dawn*, the *Tianbao* began to groan on starboard from the shear force like she was sentient.

We're not just being blown off-course. We're being crushed.

In the eye of the storm, there's an unsettling peace that works on your exhaustion, grasps past your fear, and swirls the near-empty glass of your mortal strength. It says, all of this will end. If you only give in. And it's so tempting, to linger in its false shelter.

The cloud of debris in front of the listing ship clears, and Fingers's shout jerks me back.

"There she blows!"

A flare nearly blinds us. But it's in the electric glow that we see her. All of plausibly 300 tonnes, silhouetted against a cloud of debris headed our way.

✳

On the morning of Ziyi's departure for Brani, they stood by window of the hotel, looking out onto the wave. They unfolded their arms when I stood behind them. Lifted a hand to cup my cheek.

"What if we weren't supposed to leave, but stay, and save her?"

I kissed the top of their head. "Not many mega terminals left on Earth to manage."

The panel on the bedside table pinged discreetly. Guest's shuttle to Brani leaves in an hour. Kindly ensure that you have taken all your belongings with you.

Ziyi said, "I'm putting in my reverse tender for a new contract with Brani terminal. You can join me if you want."

I don't want to fight.

"I don't know how to stop moving."

I said it to the curls of hair on their neck, but I saw the dark above Freeport's dome, where the *Constant Dawn* drifted. A locked room in a home that was never ours.

✳

There is a curious humming noise through the ship that I feel. Reverberations that ripple through my skin and bed down in the hollow of my chest, before rising to my throat. Small Fingers screams over the noise, and I grasp my mind into focus.

We got something, his lips move.

My eyes travel the length of the observation windows speckled with debris, until I see the net, blown into view by the same wind that crushes us. We got something. There, snug in the Stellamaris's Ti-alloy net, is the radio antennae of the *Constant Dawn*.

The rest of her juddering in the wind, threatening to crush us.

Small Fingers shouts through my earpiece. "You got to cut her loose."

I can't lose the *Dawn*.

"It's a gale-force storm. Lose the *Dawn* or she crushes us."

What if we weren't supposed to leave, but stay, and save her?

A moment ago, Fingers shook his head as I suited up. "You're out of your mind."

"I want to see her for myself. In any case, at this windspeed, the grip from the controls aren't responding. Someone has to go outside."

Fingers said, "That still just counts as one antenna. Smaller than my rock."

Then, the airlock is fast behind me, and the great blackness ahead. The *Constant Dawn* was bigger and more beautiful than I remembered. And worth two lifetimes on Freeport.

I realised then, I didn't know if I was going out to secure the net, or to cut it loose.

I'm screaming.

Begging Small Fingers to go back after the *Dawn* instead of cutting her loose, for me.

He shakes me. "We have to sound Mayday and hope there's a pilot at Brani's outer port limits to pick it up, if we're making it out alive," he says.

But that will reveal our unauthorised deviation. Possibly the end of deep space crewing for us. A violent jolt to the ship's side throws him, and he hits his head on the controls on the way down. He's breathing but knocked out. If I was still out in the storm, I would have been lost.

My head feels like someone is kneading their fingers on my brain.

We got something.

A rip of static crashes on me like the artificial tide on Freeport. When it ebbs, it pulls me up, off the floor. I'm back inside myself.

I reach for the comm link. "Mayday, mayday, mayday."

"Received Mayday. This is Brani Port Authority. Please state your name and situation. Over." The voice sounds familiar, but I can't process from the pain.

The line crackles and I feel the beating of my heart through my eyes.

"This is the *Tianbao*, we have sustained damage from the hurricane just beyond port limits. Request urgent assistance, and permission to call."

"Received Mayday. I'm flying out to tow you in myself. You're coming home with me, salvor," Ziyi's voice says over the line.

I can't hear myself laugh. I'm no salvor. I can't even save myself.

I don't know what I'm going back to. But I'll give us a chance to find out.

Hot Enough to Collapse

she's a camshaft—opening and closing
in precise sequence
to loosen his hand
from a fist
that's never
too late.

she's a valve—sweeping the flow
of his stomach gases,
drunken liquids
best forgotten
on a desert
runway.

she's a crankshaft—metamorphosing
linear to rotational,
high fatigue strength,
wear resistance
for maybe later,
as she waits
breathlessly
for what?

she's a spark plug—jumping the gap
to ignite the chamber
in which he sleeps
as she prepares
for the near
impossible.

she's a gasket—dressed in dust and flames,
preventing leakage
with joined objects
under compression,
as if she needs to be told
what to shovel in place.

she is a cylinder—moving up and down aquiver,
combusting fuel
that generates power
to level out
the strangeness
of being with him
as he fades
her light.

The Heavy Metal Hero, Rodney Matthews

she is a piston—tight,
converting energy
to mechanical work
so he can grunt
and whine her
to inexistence.

she's a fuel injector—atomizing fuel
into an internal engine
at a precise point
in the combustion cycle,
breathless before bracing
for his refills.

she's an exhaust—veering
his noise and fumes
from innocent bystanders
as they glance at one another,
wondering what comes next,
even as it's too late
for smart
choices.

what she needs
is an escape orbit,
a place to move away
from the source
before he makes her
a capture orbit.

what she needs
is an eclipse,
the moon passing
between earth and sun,
casting shadows
so she can remember.

what she needs
is an axis
to stabilise attitude,
and fortify the right words
more suited
to arguing.

what she needs
is a mirror
to collect light
from distant objects
in those uncertain
evenings.

so that one day
she can be hot enough
to collapse & explode
into a supernova,
a big red giant
gobbling him
into a
dwarf
star.

—*Eugen Bacon*

Colony

The soil is thin, producing
basic vegetables of slim benefit.
The air is clean they say
yet leaves you gasping
like there's a leak
in the dome … or my lungs …
my muscle's all gone, withered
and wrinkled like the blighted fruit
in the garden, if you can call it
that. I'm all for growing
lotus flowers as then we could
forget the difficulty of our ambition
and the disappointment of what we
are, and are less and less each lunar
rotation, cycle, round, and round, dizzy
ingly to think of it.
Sorry, I'm feeling light
headed like helium lifting
a balloon clear beyond
reach and up until it
becomes a dot • and
disappears from view
into space.

— A J Dalton

Space Bouncer

Your species isn't on the list –
you can't come in.
Do you even know who I am?
You can be an intergalactic overlord
for all I care: you're still not
entering, sir, madam, it, they, multiple, network
whatever.
What did you call me? How dare you,
filthy bipedal!
I'll call the Cosmic Enforcers.
Look, this has escalated
like an ill-advised snarg-hunt.
I'm sure we can come to some arrangement, no?
Perhaps my dark invasion fleet could secure you
a little moon to call your own?
Well … I did have my eye on a place,
a truly tiny planet actually
– so I'm sure no one will mind –
it's inconsequentially named
Earth.

— A J Dalton

A Grave Case of Zero Gravity

Our bones lose density
Snap to it
Our blood thins
Cuts might kill
Our bodies and minds float
Light-headed
Our focus slips sideways
Too surreal
Our thoughts widen outwards
Like unravelling
Our actions fight for purpose
Weapons set to kill
Our target seems invisible
Paranoia setting in?
We don't feel like ourselves
Sort of possessed
Till we realise they're here
In another spectrum
Entering eyes, nose, lungs
And I becomes us
All of us and other station members
Telling us to carry us
back to Earth –
so in the last moment of me
I killed them all
and now you hear us
and this trial
your trial
our trial.

— A J Dalton

Rehumanising

Branson-Musk Inc!
announces that it's eco-platforming and
doming
a Mars colony and orbiting space-bubbles
to leave only a sustainable Earth
population until the geo-nature recovers
even dinosaurs genetically reinstituted
– the rest of us will lottery-visit the planet
on short tourist-hops
and brief holi-sojourns
not like a zoo
more like a safari
without hunting though
– who'll be allowed to remain
indigenous?
wardens, gardeners, biologists
only
it's for the best
you'll see.

— A J Dalton

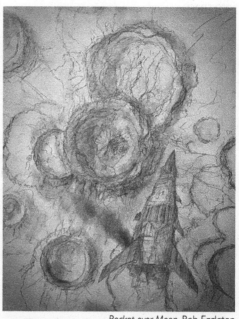

Rocket over Moon, Bob Eggleton

The Barrow King
Christopher Ruocchio

A chill wind chased through the evergreens, made them bend and scrape before the coming of the lone hunter that walked in their midst. The forest seemed to him half a temple, one built to honor some unremembered god. Above the sky was growing dark. He did not relish the thought of making the return journey—back down the craggy face of the rock—after nightfall. He did not relish the thought of making the return journey at all. Not after he did what he had come to do.

The villagers would not thank him for it, though he saved their children—and their lives.

Adaman picked his way up the slope with care, moving with the ease of long practice. He had been alone in the wilderness a long time, and was little stranger to such climbs. So much of these southern lands—where the sun was cold—was given over to such crags, to canyons, mountains, and ridges of black stone. He only wished he still had his Solva with him. She could have managed the slope with little difficulty, but the nameless horse he'd ridden more than a thousand leagues out of Hakansa would have broken a leg for certain.

He heard her nicker in the woods below, imagined she tossed her head. Looking back, he could not see her. That was well. He did not want his quarry finding her—prayed they had not heard. He had not dared leave her in the village. After all, they were *from* the village.

These men he'd come to kill.

He cleared the trees as he reached the top of the ridge, for even the hardy fir trees of the Gurrandhi Highlands could not grow in rock. There Adaman halted, surveying the world.

All the earth—which the priests of the House of Morn called *Rök*—seemed unrolled beneath him, though the mountains of the Din Gurrandh rose all around, black pillars—snow-capped—holding up the sky. He had not climbed high enough to see the Grand Wall away to the west, thousands of miles away—nor could. But he could see over the broken lands through which he'd traveled. There was the river the villagers called the Greenbend, where it flowed down out of its highland vale and ran north to join the great river that ran all the way to the Sea of Rhend. Away to the east, the land was a sheet of gnarled black stone—not the godstone of which the Walls were made—but common basalt. There the lavas flowed freely, gleaming rivers of fire steaming where they met the southern snows.

Adaman hardly saw them. His eye was drawn—as ever—to *the* eye. The God's Eye.

The red moon hung almost directly above him then, the great eye that the gods had fashioned on its face with stones vast as kingdoms peering down, forever unblinking. Seeing it filled Adaman with disquiet, as it ever did. But there—almost on the edge of sight—was a thing that fanned the little ember in his heart to old flame.

A ship. A black ship.

It moved on the upper airs, kept aloft by its twin tanks and countless rotors, like a paper dragon, black and red and gold.

He was certain that it belonged the Empire. To Qorin. His old masters. His enemy.

They're coming further south every day, he thought darkly, but put it from his mind. The Empire was far away. He had other troubles, and seeing them, pressed himself flat against the top of the ridge.

He had found them. And found the place.

Rigmardra, the locals called it. *Kingsbarrow.*

There had been kings in that country once, or so the villagers had said. Great kings and terrible. Adaman knew not what their names had been, or what name their shadowy kingdom once claimed. Had they been men, those kings? Or *neirtings, haelings,* or *elderkin?*

He did not know for certain that they'd been kings at all.

But he knew there were nine, could count them from his place on the ridgeline. An auspicious number, by the reckoning of some.

Nine were the Sons of Mor by the Great Mother, and Nine their sister-wives....

Each mound was greater than the last, each covered in a carpet of grass and wildflowers. The place might have been beautiful—placid, serene—were it not for the shadow on Adaman's heart. He knew such places, had entered into them countless times in the almost-hundred years of his too-

long life. Places of evil, where masked priests worshipped at the altars of false and dangerous gods. He knew what sort of things they intended with the boys that they had taken—and what they had already done.

Adaman knew too much of sorcery—more than any man should. Over the course of his too-long life, he'd learned to detect the stink of it. Evil had a smell, a character. He'd detected that character in the voices of the men he'd overheard whispering in the village inn that morning, in the way they put their heads together, dark eyes flitting about the smoky common room.

"It's almost time...." The big man had said, slouching into a seat not half a dozen paces from where Adaman sat, unmoving in a darkened corner. "We try again tonight."

"Tonight?" said the other—a beanpole of a fellow with beady eyes. "So soon?"

"The God's Eye is overhead. Baglan says that is well," the big man said, leaning in conspiratorially. "He says we want the God to watch."

They had spoken softly, and each in the Rhendish tongue, not the Gurrandhi spoken in the village—the better not to be understood. Though both of them had looked around, fearing to be overheard, neither had seen Adaman. Having broken his fast on bread and sausages, the hunter lingered—as he always did the morning he left such places as the village inn—to smoke his pipe in peace before he and his nameless horse set out on the next leg of their journey to nowhere.

"You found the boys?" the thin man asked, eyes darting to either side.

"Three," said the big man. Adaman could not see his face, but from the two fingers missing on his left hand, he thought he must be the village miller. Adaman had passed the mill on his way into town, a fine stone building built right on the Greenbend, its wheels turning in the rushing black water.

"Not local, are they?" the thin man hissed.

"Great Mother, no!" said the miller. "Corun bought them off a drover down in the valley night before last. He's had them up in Kingsbarrow since."

The thin man's face fell. "That means old Baglan's been at them already."

"You know the rules, Kenver," the miller said, and held up his three remaining fingers. "*Three nights.* Baglan says we have to ripen them *three nights* before we cull."

The common room had been nearly empty. Still, Adaman could scarce believe the brazenness of such men, to speak of such things in the open, in the first blush of morning, when the fog was still rolling in off the downs.

There had been no plan, no question what he must do. Adaman had simply waited for the men to leave, not stirring from his shadowed corner until they left the common room and the noise of their feet on the gravel path outside was gone. The witches who had made Adaman what he was had sharpened his hearing so that almost he could see the two men reach the end of the gravel path and turn in opposite directions when they reached the muddy high street that formed the spine of the village called Glastag, Greenhome.

Adaman had had no need to follow them.

Everyone in the village knew where Rigmardra was....

... where the barrows were.

The locals avoided the place like a lazaret. It was haunted, they said, by the shades of the old kings, their vavasors and bannermen, their concubines and slaves ... and by men such as the miller and the thin one called Kenver.

Sorcerers.

Coming back to himself, Adaman saw one of his quarry, and pressed himself flat to the earth atop the ridge overlooking the valley where the barrows stood.

The sorcerer was seated on a stone at the base of the largest mound, beside what appeared to be the mouth of the tumulus—a great, uneven black arch. The foul magus wore a cloak of animal skins over his commoner's weeds, with a deep hood that covered the eyes. To the untrained eye, he might have seemed a part of the wilderness. But to Adaman, he seemed to glow.

"Adram," the hunter prayed, invoking his own god, the god of demise and destruction, of cleansing fire. The god of warriors; of death; and of new life again, after. "Lord God, guide your servant. May my hand be swift. May my blade be sure. Do this, and I will make an offering to you: the deaths of these men. Their blood for the blood they have taken. Their lives for the lives they've unmade. Make of me your vengeance. Make of me your blade."

Slowly then, Adaman raised himself from the earth. Remaining on his knees a moment, he saluted the setting sun—for the sun was Adram's, whatever the priests of Mor and his harlot might say.

It was right that he should come upon them at twilight, for sunset was Adram's hour.

This would be Adram's day.

Standing, Adaman darted along the ridge, right hand steadying the great blade slung over his shoulder, left on the hilt of the common sword at his waist. The magus had not seen him. The man had some weapon out across his knees. A crossbow, maybe, or an arbalest.

There were at least four men, Adaman knew. The big miller—whose name he did not know—the thin Kenver, and Corun, and Baglan. There could be more, and many more. Adaman knew not how many, nor had he any notion of just how great the mages' magick might be. In his day, he'd known sorcerers strong enough to raise the dead, great enough to bend light and time itself. But others he had known had no power at all, only dreamed of power, or else pretended to it.

And men did not need power to be dangerous.

But Adaman had a power of his own.

Coming to a place where the descent was steepest, Adaman leaped, still holding his swords to stop them rattling in their scabbards. It was half a hundred feet to the valley floor.

Adaman landed lightly as a feather.

Still the magus had not seen him. That was well.

The valley was a long, deep cut, with stone walls high on either side, one of many scoured across the highlands by the retreat of glaciers in the Dawn, when Rök was forged. All the world had been sheathed in ice— so it was said. All agreed it would be sheathed in ice once more, when the sun went out, though none agreed when that day would come.

The last and greatest of the nine barrows lay at the head of that valley, not a free-standing mound, but a hillock piled against the head of the valley proper. The grass that carpeted the valley grew to half the height of a man, had gone gray and brittle with the press of coming winter, had grown in patchy tussocks like a boy's first growth of beard. Still, it was enough to conceal him.

Almost enough.

The magus saw him, scrambled to his feet.

The fool forgot to cry out, raised his arbalest. Fired.

Fast as the bolt was, Adaman was faster. He drew his sword—the common sword that hung from his belt—and slashed the bolt from the air before it could strike his face. The shaft spun away to the right. The sorcerer stood no chance of reloading. He barely dropped the crossbow before Adaman was on him. Adaman left him no time to so much as draw his knife.

One hand on the pommel for added force, Adaman thrust the curving sword into the mage's black heart. The hunter ran the man back into the steep face of the hill, sword caught between his ribs. Adaman felt the shock of impact as the man struck the hill, felt his blade pass through the man and pierce the hill itself.

The bright ring of metal on metal filled the air. That surprised Adaman, but he kept his focus. Red blood ran from the mage's mouth. The hand that had gone for his knife fumbled. Adaman did not take his eyes from the sorcerer's face. The old familiar rage—kindled by the sight of that Imperial airship—had caught in his belly.

The Lion's Dog, that was what they'd called him.

But that was so, so long ago.

The magus sagged. His teeth bared, Adaman did not take his eyes from the wizard's face until the light had left his eyes. Then Adaman stood, looked up at the black arch overhead. It was not stone, as he had suspected. Standing over the body of the slain sorcerer, he reached out, touched the lip of the door into darkness.

It was metal.

His ears had not deceived him.

The toothless hag that had sold him dried meat and bread for the road—the woman who had told him of Rigmardra in the first place—had told him that the barrow-builders laid their kings in their ships, sealed and buried whole vessels in the highlands. Ships were more common in those days, so Adaman had always heard. Still, he had scarce believed it. It seemed madness to him. A waste.

A shout and a cry sounded from deep within, shook Adaman from his study of the gate.

Adaman had ventured into such places a thousand times before, into the deep places of the world, where the light of the sun—Adram's light—did not reach, save what little he brought with him. He did not fear the darkness, nor what lay in that darkness.

It would be made to fear him.

Common sword in hand, he cros-

sed the threshold, felt a dry wind lift his weather-stained cloak, tug his long, dark hair back from his bronze face. The ground beneath his feet was uneven, for the passage of so many years had carried the earth into the chamber, sloping down toward a round inner door. The roof above was all of ridged black metal, sloping down to meet that inner gate. By the end, Adaman could almost touch it.

Another cry sounded from inside, and the rough voice of a man before the cry was choked off. Fearing he was too late, Adaman forged past the inner gate, entered a chamber like a tube, the floor roundly flowing into walls and ceiling, the all of it clad in dark metal. Each step rang brightly, despite the hunter's best intentions.

"The cord, Corun!" A man's voice floated from within. "Hold him down!"

Adaman halted at the next door, peered through it. The hall within was canted at a shallow angle, rising to the left, sinking to the right. The ancient highlanders who had entombed the ship in the barrow had not leveled it properly. The sorcerers had set rushlights along the floor, and hung charms from the sloping ceiling, chimes wrought of hollow bone. Careful not to disturb them, Adaman wove his way down the hall, careful to make as little sound as he was able.

The sorcerers had clearly been in that place a long time. As he reached the end of the hall and came to the next he saw a bank of tallow candles lighted along the opposite wall, their fat running in tendrils down the wall to puddle on the floor. More bones were set among them. Skulls. Thighbones. Pelvises. More of the bone chimes hung from the ceiling, hands held together by lengths of twine. On more than one, Adaman saw the blackened remains of what had been little ears, set up to listen for the approach of foes.

Such charms were false magic. There was no power in them.

That made them all the more terrible.

"Hold him down, I said!"

The hunter reached the final gate, and peering round its jamb saw the inner sanctum, the tomb of the barrow king. The room was broad and open, high ceiling barrel-vaulted, walls lined with shoals of melting candles, decorated with bone.

Standing in the center of the far wall was a coffin of iron and clear glass. Within it, the mummified remains of a body lay, utterly desiccated, skin dark as onyx, long hair white as snow. Of gold were the rings upon its fingers, its armlets, anklets, and the necklaces it yet wore. Of gold, too, was the circlet set upon its once-noble brow, set with square-cut rubies.

It was the barrow king, its body still intact, unspoiled by looters despite its having languished there for long millennia. The body had the look of the elderkin about it: the black skin; the pale hair; the long, pointed ears. Had the Eternal ruled these lands in days of old?

Perhaps the toothless woman in Glastag knew his name, or knew his kingdom, or knew how to count the long years since his dominion.

Perhaps no one did.

No one, that is, save the cult of pagan worshippers kneeling before his tomb.

There were eight—the man on the door, the man Adaman had already killed—made nine.

Nine were the Sons of Mor by the Great Mother, and Nine their sister-wives....

"Maelung!" they chanted, all as one. "Maelung! Maelung! Lord and lover!"

"Lord and lover!" their leader cried.

"Lord and lover!" the others echoed.

Maelung? Adaman thought.

Maelung was one of Mor's nine sons, the demigod king of Cahaen, one of the Nine Kingdoms of Rök in its Dawn. But Cahaen was far away, they said—if it ever existed—and far to the west, beyond the Grand Wall. Farther than any man of Rhend had ever traveled, farther than any ship of Qorin had ever sailed. He could not be buried in the highlands of the bitter south, nor in so drab a tomb.

These fool pagan sorcerers were deluded.

But even delusions were perilous where magick was concerned—and perhaps especially delusions.

"Lord, hear us!" the headman— no doubt the man called Baglan— called. "Drink the blood that we have brought you! Look upon our sacrifice with kindness! Return as we have returned! To you! To life! To Rök!"

They were naked, every one of them, though each wore masks of bone. They each had daubed themselves with soot collected from the burning rushlights, or else with lime. Each had painted patterns on their flesh, on the flesh of one another. They knelt in half a circle before the tomb, hands raised. In their midst, on a woven blanket of red and white, lay the three boys they had bought off their highland drover. The oldest no more than ten.

They were bound, bruised, gagged.

"Maelung! Maelung! Maelung!" the men intoned.

The headman raised the instrument of sacrifice—a needle bound to a length of braided hose. The others continued their chant, breathing the name of the Son of Mor to a drumbeat only they could hear.

The headman spoke, singing:

Lord of Flesh, of Love, of Gold
sleep no more in dark and cold.
Drink the blood that we have shared.
Take the sacrifice prepared.
Lord of Flesh, of Love, of Gold
sleep no more in dark and cold.
Walk once more in light of day,
drive our enemies away.
Lord of Flesh, of Love, of Gold
sleep no more in dark and cold ...

Adaman wished that he'd had the sense to bring the watchman's arbalest. He might have taken one in the back from the safety of the inner door. He stood transfixed, unable to move, unable to look away, as the headman—Baglan—thrust the needle into the first boy's shuddering neck. There was no blood. The blood was in the hose, the coiling thread that ran from the bound sacrifice to the glass sarcophagus that held the sleeping barrow king. For the first time, Adaman marked the witch-lights that shone in the wall beside the tomb of the ancient king, blue and white.

Adaman understood.

They meant to flush the child's blood into the corpse in the glass coffin, and so stir it to new life. Such a thing was possible, if the corpse had been rightly mummified—and this one had.

But Adaman had seen enough.

His horror found his courage, his courage his rage.

Not bothering to muffle his footsteps, he strode across the floor of that black sanctum.

Too late, the mages turned, and saw him standing over them: the tall Numorran, black-haired, bronze-faced, stern and scarred. Beneath his faded cloak, he wore a quilted gambeson, once black, now gray-green. Greaves wrapped his long legs, and he wore a vambrace on his right arm—but it was the left that drew the eye. The gauntlet, pauldron, and manica that sheathed that arm was white as bone, as ivory, a jointed construction of delicate plates—claw-like—that moved as he moved.

It was this hand that seized the nearest sorcerer, grasping him by the throat. The pale arm gleamed with witchlights of its own, and at Adaman's command a bolt of lightning coursed through the mage's flabby flesh. Only after he fell smoking did Adaman recognize the nameless miller.

His curving sword flashed then, cutting right then left. With each stroke he tore the throats from the men to the miller's either side. The others, startled, scrambled back, grubby in their nakedness. One, a big man and stronger than the rest, rose clutching the knife that he'd intended to cut the throats of their victims when all was done. Tall though Adaman was, this magus was taller, broader.

He lunged, but Adaman parried his knife with ease, hewed at the big

Myrmidon, Bruce Pennington

man's arm. Blood spattered the metal floor, and the big man staggered back, tearing the mask from his face to better see. Adaman recognized the man from the smithy that had reshod his nameless horse.

"You!" the big man said. "What are you—you should have minded your own business!"

Adaman said nothing.

They were ordinary men. That was the worst part.

All of them.

Ordinary men.

The man passed the knife from one hand to the other, lunged again. Adaman beat the knife from his hand with his own blade, pressed forward. The big man staggered back, tripped over the boys they'd laid out for sacrifice.

A shot lanced past Adaman then, red in that dark place. The shot went wide, and Adaman rounded on the sorcerer who had cast it. The others had all gathered weapons laid about the tomb, bright swords with pale blades and gilded handles, golden wands with eyes of flame.

One such eye lanced at him again, caught Adaman in the shoulder. He snarled, rounded on the man. The mage's next shot went wide, and Adaman leaped at him, knocking the wand from the wizard's hand before he rammed his blade into the man's black heart.

It was the thin man from the inn, the one called Kenver.

"Stop!" the headman was on his feet, face concealed by the face of a skull too small for him, his body coated with lime, dark hair wild. In his hands he clutched a weapon of the Dawn, like a crossbow without the bow. Its stock was horn, its body gilded steel, its price beyond the reckoning of princes.

And its shot was death.

"Name yourself!" the wizard said.

"Baglan," Adaman guessed, and from the way the naked sorcerer shuffled, he knew that he had guessed rightly, "you cannot raise the dead. Not like this."

Blood red as the finest vermillion glowed in the cord that ran from the eldest child. They were wasting time. Four of the mages yet lived.

"That is what you think!" Baglan said, shouldering the arquebus. "We have quickened their blood by torment. Three nights beneath the God's Eye. We have said the proper words. Done the proper deeds. Lord Maelung will rise again!"

"That isn't Maelung," Adaman said, not lowering his sword. "That is some mountain king of the elderkin! Are you blind?"

"You know nothing!" Baglan said. "Your little mind can scarce conceive what it is we do."

Adaman's eyes went to the boys lying on the floor. One was surely dead, already exsanguinated. Well he knew the bite of the witch's needle. Well he recalled the pits of Magoth. His collar. Azara's bed. "I know *exactly* what it is you do."

Such was the tenor of his voice that Baglan faltered. The arquebus drooped—if only for an instant. "Who are you?"

Adaman did not answer.

"That *thing*, on your arm," Baglan said. "It is god-make."

Still Adaman was silent.

"Give it to me!" the headman said. The other mages had spread out, formed an arc around and before the lonely hunter.

Four men, Adaman counted. His shoulder ached where the wand had taken him. *Only four.*

"Name yourself!"

When still the hunter said nothing, Baglan aimed his arquebus over Adaman's shoulder. Fired. The shot split the dark chamber like a wedge, bright as the rising sun.

"Speak!"

Adaman only stared.

"Kill him, Baglan!" said the big man, clutching his wounded arm. "We'll feed his blood to the god!"

"Kill him!"

"Kill him now!"

Baglan shouldered the ancient weapon, aimed it square at Adaman's chest.

He never got the chance to fire.

An unseen hand slammed into him, knocked the weapon back and upward. The shot sliced the ceiling, and Adaman seized his moment, rushing in, sword drawn back for the thrust. His curving blade plunged into Baglan's belly, and the headman stumbled back, heel catching on the dais at the base of the glass sarcophagus. He fell, and Adaman's sword was almost wrenched from his hand as he fell. The hunter staggered, and as he staggered, he felt the bite of a blade in his own back. Red pain flooded his senses, and he cursed, turning, found the big man staring down at him.

"Careful, Corun!" said one of the others. "He uses magick!"

Adaman stretched his eyes wide, and a shout of force hurled the big man from him, clear across the crypt. The hunter's whole body went cold,

colder than his meager blood loss could account for. The power sucked the life from him, drew from the fire in his blood.

The knife was still in him.

He had to draw it out if the healing was to begin.

If he drew it out, he would have a weapon.

Reaching back behind himself, he found the bone hilt of the mage's dagger, tugged it free.

"What is he?" asked one of the mages, drawing back. "A witch?"

Boom.

The sound rose from deep in the bowels of the buried vessel. A hollow, metallic boom, as if the bolt of some almighty door were unlocked.

"What was that?" asked one of the naked men.

Cold laughter bubbled up behind Adaman, and he looked back, half-expecting to find Baglan still alive, clinging to life by some fell art. But the flabby magus was dead, his blood red upon the dais. Horrified, Adaman turned to regard the corpse in its glass sarcophagus.

The children's blood had not stirred the mummy to new life.

A voice—deep and black as the underworld—filled the chamber, seemingly issued from its walls. Its words seemed to Adaman to be the speech of the elderkin, but he could not understand it. He understood its meaning plain enough. *You do not belong here,* it seemed to say. *You should not have come.*

"Maelung!" one of the sorcerers cried. "Lord and lover, god!"

Already Adaman could feel the sinews in his back beginning to knit. The witches had given him that gift, at least. The bleeding had surely stopped. He dropped the bone-handled knife, placed one hand on the baldric slung over his shoulder, the other on the hilt of the great sword slung over his back.

He had hoped not to need it.

It was a famous blade.

If word got back to Qorin, or to Parha, or the Wall, that the White Sword had been seen in the highlands beyond Rhend, the Empire would surely send its ships.

But word would not get out.

Doors opened in the rear of the crypt, one to either side of the dead and dreamless king.

With his heightened sense, Adaman surely saw them first.

Tall they were, taller than any mortal men—tall as the lords of the elderkin in ancient days before the fall. Black-skinned were they as their makers, limbs bound in rings of gold, their fleshless bodies painted with intricate designs, the like of which Baglan's crude markings were only the faintest, foulest imitation. They were clad each only in breechclouts of white silk, time-eaten and frayed.

There were two of them, each holding a hooked and wicked blade.

Adaman knew what they were at once. Barrow-dwellers. Again-walkers. Wights. The deathless servants of their long-dead king. Their flesh was iron. Their hearts steel.

Adaman unfastened his baldric, unslung the White Sword. It was one of the Namsarí, forged in Adom, in Godhome, for Mor's faithful knights.

It was, perhaps, the last Namsar in all creation.

And Adaman drew it forth, and lo! It was broken a foot from the tip, so that its end came a jagged point. Still, it was longer than any sword had a right to be. Longer, broader, sharper ... still lighter than any steel. The blade glowed in the dim candlelight, white as virgin snow.

Dropping his sword, one of the naked mages rushed forward, dropped to his knees before the wight, hands pawing at its breechclout. "We are your servants!" he said. "Your slaves! We are yours! Do with us as you—"

... *please.*

He never finished.

The wight's crooked sword took off his head. In a single motion, it turned its flat-nosed face on Adaman, long white mane swaying. His shoulder ached where the big mage had knifed him, his body ached from his use of the witch's power. Still Adaman raised the Namsar of Godhome, held it high in challenge.

Faster than human seeing, the wight lunged at him. Adaman brought his sword slamming down, felt the blade connect. The White Sword needed no sharpening, for no stone could make it sharper than the forges of Godhome already had. It could cut anything and never dull, for nothing could blunt its edge, nor break it—save the one thing that had.

The wight's blade fell in two pieces, and the iron demon had no recourse but to batter Adaman aside. Its fellow moved with great speed, its sword cleaving the other mage in two near as easily as if the weapon were a Namsar itself.

The big man with the wounded arm—the last of Baglan's foul brood—turned and made for the door. He could not have gone more than three paces before the wight overtook him, and opened him from shoulder to groin.

Adaman hit the wall, knocked skull and candles to the floor. The wight whose sword he had destroyed advanced on him, moving slowly, threateningly. The black voice was still speaking, filling the chamber with its malice. With a cry and a shout of power, Adaman lunged. His will staggered the fell creature, lifted bones and candles and tattered clothing from the ground. The Namsar flashed, clove through the wight's black hide, split its iron bones and golden bangles.

It fell at Adaman's feet, and the objects his will had lifted fell with it.

A dreadful cold leeched through the hunter then, and he faltered. The second wight rounded on him, moving with a speed and terrible vengeance. It was all Adaman could do to raise his sword in time, even with his more-than-human reflexes. His parry severed the monster's arm entire, and its crooked sword fell with nerveless fingers. Undaunted, unfeeling, the wight pummeled Adaman with its other hand, and the hunter skidded across the floor, head ringing. The Namsar fell from his hand, and the one-handed wight loomed over him. It grabbed at him, and Adaman grabbed at it—grabbed it with his left hand.

Lighting coursed once more through the godforged armor, poured into the monster as it stooped to seize him. It fell smoking just beside him.

The rest was silence.

Adaman lay there only a moment. He had forgotten the boy. Almost forgotten. Shivering, aching, battered and bloody, he limped across the floor to the three boys. The one was certainly dead, the second dying. He untied him as gently as his fumbling hands would allow. Applying pressure, Adaman drew out the witch's needle. "Keep your hand here," he said. "Press hard. You understand?"

The sight of him fanned the fury in Adaman's guts once more, and he untied the third boy. Neither had it in them to move... not after all that they had suffered.

"*You,*" the black voice said, speaking the common tongue.

Adaman looked up, looked into the face of the long-dead barrow king.

"*You are witchmarked,*" the dead king said, voice filling the chamber.

The two boys shuddered.

"You should be dead," Adaman said. "You are no *haeling*; your bones should not remember."

The barrow king did not move, nor did he give any sign.

"*Our will endures,*" he said, voice emanating from the room entire. "*We endure. Our spirit preserved in light and crystal.*"

Adaman said nothing. The Namsar lay not far from where he knelt with the poor victims. He found his feet. He had heard of sorcerers trapping their spirits in crystal to escape death. He had never seen it done.

"*You are witchmarked,*" the barrow king said once more. "*We see the shadow on you ... Numorran. The weight ...*"

Adaman could feel the witch-king's fingers in his mind, saw his memories as the dead thing lifted them, turned them in his hands. The grottoes of Magoth. His collar. His chains. The witch's needle. Her lust. Her blood on his hands.

"*You need not bear it alone,*" the barrow king said. "*Let us bear it for you. Take it from you.*"

There were two suns in the sky, red and white. Numor. His home. The world he no longer remembered. His father's face. His mother's tears.

"You need but take us out of here," the monster said. *"And we will bear your memory. Ease your pain."*

He leaped from the deck of a Qorinese airship, caught the rigging with one hand. The ship was going down in fire. The earth rushing up to meet it. He shoved the memories away, but every time he tried, the wight seized another, presented each to him in turn. Adaman shut his eyes, but shutting them did not stop the visions.

"You will be a king," the barrow king said, *"as we were of old...."*

Winged Lion banners flew beneath the standard of the Parhan King. "Samar!" the men all cried. "Samar! Samar!"

"Samar ..."

Adaman felt his hair floating from his shoulders, felt the power gather in his chest.

He took a step, and the metal of the floor broke beneath him. The crack traveled, reached the casket and the body of the barrow king. Glass shattered, bones splintered, and the witchlights around the sarcophagus sputtered and died.

Adaman's hands were shaking, with fury and with cold.

He had not heard the hated name, not in years. Not in decades.

He had never wanted to hear it again.

He carried the boys one by one from the barrow, fed them, clothed them. It would be days before they spoke. He would not take them back to Glastag—for all he knew, there were yet more of Baglan's coven in the place, more monsters in man's shape. While the boys ate and shivered by the fire, Adaman gathered the riches of the barrow and laid them on the grass outside. Knives and swords there were, and rings, bangles, bracelets ... cups and plates and drinking horns. Then there were the crystals, great sheets of diamond shot through with flaws by the mage's art. He had shattered them into pieces, and set the pieces in the sun. Let men find them, take them, make other men cut them down for jewelry. With every cut, the spirit of the barrow king would be destroyed a little more, until ten thousand little pearls of his awareness remained in the coronets of queens and on the hands of merchant's wives.

The arquebus Adaman kept for himself.

He set aside parcels for both the boys. Enough—and more than enough—to buy them some proper home. An apprenticeship. A new life.

When the sun rose once more in the north, Adaman set the boys both upon his nameless horse, and turned them all to face it. He would take them north, far from Glastag and the highlands, far from the horror they had faced.

In his secret heart, he prayed a prayer of thanks to Adram—whose sun it was.

Together then, they left Rigmardra, never to return.

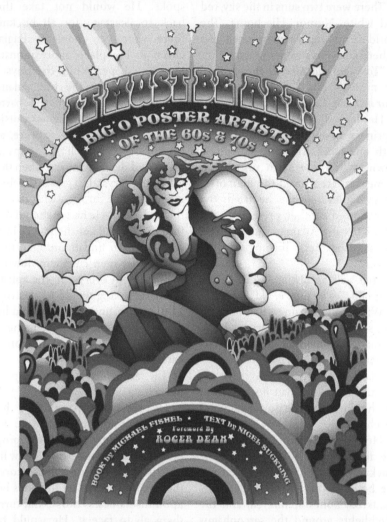

It Must Be Art : Big O Poster Artists of the 1960s and 70s
Michael Fishel and Nigel Suckling

Throughout the 1960s and 70s, London-based Big O Posters helped define the new and
democratic art medium of the psychedelic poster, a vehicle for rebellion against the old order
that went hand in hand with the music, literature, and film of the time. This is a
comprehensive collection of works published by Big O artists, astonishingly creative folks
whose artistry developed almost completely outside the influence of the art establishment.
Included in more than 300 images are works by 19 artists, including Martin Sharp, Roger Dean,
H.R. Giger, Robert Venosa, and Vali Myers, whose signature styles include sci-fi, fantasy,
visionary, botanical, and surrealism. In addition to hundreds of original works, this book digs
below the surface to offer insights and anecdotes about the era, the artistic process, and reveals
connections to artists from the past (Aubrey Beardsley, Alphonse Mucha, Kay Nielsen) whose
spirit chimed with the age of Big O Posters.

Size: 8.5in x 11.0in | Pages: 304 | 300+ colour & b/w images
Binding: Hardback | Publisher: Schiffer Books
ISBN: 9780764355486
PRICE: $50.00

The Secret Sharer

Robert Silverberg

Illustrated by Tom Canty

Signed, Limited Edition
ISBN: 978-1-64524-145-4 • 160 pages • $60

An Interview with Robert Silverberg

Justin T. O'Conor Sloane

Sloane: Bob, I am honored that you agreed to do this interview. Thank you! When did your lifelong interest in science fiction begin?

Silverberg: When I was about ten, and I discovered Verne's *Twenty Thousand Leagues Under the Sea* and Wells's *The Time Machine*. I don't remember which came first. Perhaps the real starting point was age seven, when I was reading Planet Comics.

When did you begin writing in earnest?

I learned how to read before I was four and was writing immediately. I had things published in my school newspaper when I was six, in the first grade. There never was a time when I wasn't a writer.

When did you get your first story published?

I think it was 1952, in a magazine called *The Avalonian*. (The first one for which I got paid, anyway. I had some in fanzines before that.)

When did you decide that writing was the career for you?

I expected to be a scientist of some sort, perhaps a paleontologist. But when I was about twelve, in junior high school, the teacher in charge of a vocational-guidance session said, "Your parents think you're going to be a writer." That startled me. I had always been writing, yes, but it had never occurred to me to make a career out of it. Thanks to that push—the teacher's name was Miss Kogut, and I guess she had been talking to my parents at some parent-teacher meeting—I began thinking right then and there about whether I could make a

career out of writing. It turned out that I could.

When did you know that you could be successful as a science fiction writer?

I sold a few stories in 1953 and 1954. But suddenly in the summer of 1955 I sold a whole lot of them and it became clear to me that I could really do it.

You have had a remarkably distinguished and productive career as a science fiction writer. I often wonder how especially successful people accomplish so much in their field of endeavor. Can you provide us with some insight relating to this and to your own journey as a writer?

All I can say is that I very much wanted to be a science-fiction writer, I worked at it, I read a lot of stuff and studied it closely, I wrote a lot of stuff, and, well, from the time I was 21 on I got where I wanted to go. It's easy to say, "Go and do the same," but I have no idea how easy it is to do. In retrospect it seems that I had a pretty easy time but I remember lots of rejections in the early years.

Further to this, if you had to choose one attribute, quality, or characteristic that you have found to be the most useful to achieving your success as a science fiction writer, what would it be?

Persistence. And some degree of verbal skill.

I've long considered science fiction to be a generational thought experiment, one in which we create blueprints for an imagined, yet possible, future replete with challenges and solutions. In this way, do you think that science fiction can be used as a tool for the betterment of human existence through speculation? Can we in fact influence our future reality through this literature?

I don't have an answer to this one. I was just a storyteller. I never thought much about bettering human existence by making up fantastic stories.

You've been writing science fiction for a very long time now. What are some of the most noteworthy changes that you have witnessed in this field?

The shift from magazine-centered publishing to paperback-centered publishing was a very big thing in the early years of my career. When I was starting out, there were lots of magazines, most of them hungry for material; only Ace and Ballantine (now Del Rey) were important paperback markets, but soon there were a great many, whereas the numerous magazines began to vanish around 1958. On the other hand, the overwhelming success of the Tolkien books led to the trilogy phenomenon, and these days it is very hard for a stand-alone SF novel to get any attention. I don't regard this as a good thing. The trilogy may have worked for Asimov, but it's not an ideal form for science fiction.

Do you like the new stuff? Any favorites? Anything you'd like to see being done that isn't being done?

I don't pay much attention to current SF. I think I've read enough of the stuff for one lifetime. Occasionally I go back to an old favorite like Vance or Dick or Kuttner, but I don't keep up with the modern field.

You once said that you consider the 1950s to be the true Golden Age of science fiction. Why?

The important writers of the 1950s—Vance, Bester, Dick, Clarke, Leiber, Sheckley, Blish, Kornbluth, Pohl, Knight, Sturgeon, Budrys, and a number of others—built on the work done by van Vogt, Simak, Heinlein, Williamson, De Camp, and the rest of John Campbell's crew of the early 1940s, but added an extra degree of literary sophistication that greatly expanded the idea of what science fiction could do. And the Ballantine paperback series alone, giving us *More Than Human* and *Bring the Jubilee* and *The Space Merchants* and *Fahrenheit 451* and *Childhood's End* all in one giddy rush, was a Golden Age all in itself.

When Bob Silverberg reads science fiction, who does he read?

As stated above. Old stuff, mostly.

Do you believe that the human imagination, at the individual level, can be trained to attain higher levels of creative thought?

I don't have a good answer for this, except to say that I hope so.

Inspiration fuels the human imagination, generating ideas and driving us to create. Where do natural talent and an iron-willed work ethic come into play?

These are the three foundations of any successful writing career. There have been plenty of one-hit wonders who have turned out the occasional masterpiece, but one needs to have all three qualities in order to make a lifetime enterprise of it.

If the easy energy from inspiration drops off during a writing project, what is the remedy?

Inspiration is the least important part of it. Seat of the pants in the chair and fingers on the keyboard matter more.

Is writing a joyous process for you? Has it ever felt like a form of drudgery?

Of course it has. But if it felt like drudgery all the time, I would have been crazy to keep at it for sixty years, and whatever else I am, I'm not crazy.

Any words of advice for emerging writers who hope to become a household name in science fiction?

Keep at it, is all I can say. It worked for me.

Did you learn something as a writer the really hard way? Anything you'd share with us about this?

When I was young and batting out pulp stories at a great rate (and selling them all) H. L. Gold of *Galaxy* sent me a stinging rejection slip asking me if that was all I meant to do with my obvious talent. I wasn't hurt by it. I realized that what he was saying made sense, and it shook me up in a good way. Not much later, Lester del Rey, who had become a friend and a kind of Dutch uncle to me, pointed out that although I was selling everything I wrote, most of what I was writing would never be reprinted in an anthology, and that all I would earn from it was my initial payment, whereas better material went on and on in many editions—so even if all I was interested in doing was making money from my writing, I was going about it the wrong way. It was, I think, the best writing advice I ever had.

Did writing come easy to you?

Sometimes yes, sometimes no. I have at times gleefully reeled off thousands of words with hardly a pause for breath. At other times I've spent hours wondering what the next word ought to be. It varies.

Any recommendations on how to become a better writer?

Read a lot. Write a lot.

After winning prestigious science fiction prizes, did anything change in your approach to your writing and to your literary career?

No. I was, of course, glad to win some Hugos and Nebulas. But each new story was a challenge in its own right, which had to be approached in its own way, and whatever awards I had won in the past would have no effect on the new task. When I won the most prestigious award of all, the SFWA Grand Master trophy, I was nearing the end of my writing career, and getting that one was more of a validation of what I had already done than an impetus to do anything new.

It seems that science fiction is more popular than it has ever been, now reaching a very large and established mainstream audience through film, television, online, and print. Do you think that the genre will ever reach a saturation point?

I hope not.

Science fiction is well suited to the exploration of various social and political issues. Do you prefer science fiction that is grounded in the issues and provides robust social and political commentary, or science fiction that is decoupled from the sociology and instead explores wholly new worlds and marvels of advanced technology?

The latter. Social and political commentary becomes stale very fast, unless it's on the level of Orwell's 1984. A story like van Vogt's "Black Destroyer," written more than eighty years ago, has no political content whatever, but still holds power for today's reader. Science fiction closely linked to today's headlines quickly becomes as interesting as last month's newspaper.

What should a science fiction writer do every day for success?

Get up. Eat breakfast. Write something.

Are you still writing new material? If not, why is this so?

I'm 89 years old. Time for a rest. Very few writers have achieved much in old age, and I don't want to find out that I can't.

What do you think your greatest contributions to the literary canon of science fiction are?

Not for me to say. I know which stories I'm most proud to have written, but I would be patting myself on my back if I talked about them openly. I think I did make some important contributions, but I'd rather let others decide which they were.

Is there anything that you would have done differently in your literary career?

No. I might have gone in for writing trilogies, or for doing fantasy novels, or jumping on other bandwagons, but what I did do worked out well and I'm happy to have achieved what I did.

Did you have a consistent routine as a writer? If so, anything you'd like to share? What worked best for you?

I got to my desk about 8 every morning and worked steadily until noon, Monday through Friday, an invariable routine. I never answered the telephone during those hours and, of course, there was no Internet to distract me then. In the early very prolific years I would go back to work after lunch and do another stint until three, but I stopped that around 1970. I stuck to that routine right until the end of my career.

Do you prefer dystopian or optimistic science fiction?

No preference here. A good story is what I look for, period.

So much of what has been written in science fiction about the future has come to pass—

especially technological developments. Why do you think that is?

The pace of technological development has been accelerating ever since the invention of the stone axe. Things are happening faster and faster all the time. Some science-fiction themes are still not reality, because they are basically impossible (time travel, faster-than-light speeds, telepathy) but whatever can actually be developed is being developed as fast as possible.

You have been a reader and collector of science fiction magazines, from the pulps to the slicks, for most of your life. Which are your favorites? Which ones inspired and influenced you the most?

Astounding Science Fiction of the 1939–52 John W. Campbell era had a profound effect on me, as did Horace Gold's *Galaxy*, 1950–55. I also was much influenced by *Startling Stories* and *Thrilling Wonder Stories* in the last few years of their existence before they disappeared in 1955. A great ambition of mine destined never to be fulfilled is to send some of my best stories back in time so that they could be published in some of those splendid magazines of yesteryear.

What is your favorite science fiction novel written by another author? Your favorite SF movie? SF television show? Who are some of your favorite SF authors?

I can't pick a favorite SF novel, I don't see a great many SF movies, and I know next to nothing about SF television shows. My favorite SF authors include Vance, Dick, Sheckley, Blish, Bester, Kuttner, Leiber, van Vogt, and maybe half a dozen others that don't hop immediately to mind.

As a science fiction author and historian,

which do you consider to be some of the best and most influential ideas found in the literary canon of science fiction? How about some of the worst—even when very influential?

This one is too broad for me to deal with here, except to say that the early novels of H. G. Wells are surely the most influential works of the canon (*The Time Machine, The War of the Worlds, The Island of Doctor Moreau, The Invisible Man,* and a couple of others.) His short stories are important too.

Which organization do you credit with being most beneficial to the field of science fiction?

I helped to found the Science Fiction Writers of America (I was its second president, in 1967 and 1968) and I think its early work was quite beneficial. I don't follow its activities very closely these days.

Which of your books do you think did the most for your career? Why?

Nightwings put me on the map with a Hugo. *Dying Inside* helped to establish my literary credentials, and *Lord Valentine's Castle* restored my commercial viability after a period of declining sales.

Do you have a favorite book or story that you have written, whether outright or from a particular period of your writing?

I do, but the answer fluctuates from time to time, so I'll take a pass on this one.

Which of your books was the hardest to write? Why?

I think *At Winter's End*, because it required me to invent a very complex future history and keep a huge cast of characters in mind. I had all sorts of charts to guide me through.

Which of your books felt the easiest to write? Why?

I'm stumped here. Each book had its easy moments and its tough moments.

Has there been a particular publisher that you liked working with the most?

Doubleday, I think, when Larry Ashmead was its editor. My career was just entering its mature period and he gave me great encouragement with each project. Lou Aronica of Bantam was another editor I enjoyed working with. For short stories, Alice Turner of *Playboy* was a superb playmate, always leading me to improve what was actually pretty good in the first place.

Any emerging science fiction authors that you are keeping an eye on particularly?

Nope. Not really keeping up these days.

Who were some authors, in science fiction or any genre, that most influenced you?

Outside of SF, Graham Greene, Joseph Conrad, William Faulkner. (Among others). The SF authors who most influenced me are the ones I listed as favorites above.

Do you think that science fiction is more imaginative now, or is it ultimately much the same fundamentally, but reflecting a larger body of scientific knowledge, advances in technology, new cultural influences, a grand flourishing of women SF writers, and an ever-evolving pool of ideas?

Again, this one is too broad for me to deal with.

Has science fiction evolved as you thought it might?

Not really. I didn't expect all these trilogies, all this space opera, all the return to pulp tropes. I thought we were heading in a more literary direction.

Do you think that today's science fiction is moving in a new direction? If so, is that reflective of an organic evolution that certainly includes, but is not entirely driven by, changes in society and an overarching intentionality for the genre?

My impression is that today's science fiction is trying too hard to address current issues (racism, sexism, etc.) and that is likely to drive away readers who are looking for more visionary material. But of course I'm not keeping up with the new stuff, so all I can go by is the list of award winners. As for changes in society, yes, there have been changes in society, all right, that are taking us away from uninhibited free speech, and if I were writing today I would feel uncomfortable about that.

T, Paulo Sayeg

What function do you think science fiction plays in society? Is its role simply one of providing entertainment and escapism coupled with the rush produced by some really exciting ideas?

That is indeed what I think. There's the old line, "If you have a message, take it to Western Union." Stories ought to be about something, yes, but they shouldn't be lectures.

If you could change one thing about today's science fiction scene, what would it be?

I'd take it back to where it was when I began reading it seventy-plus years ago. But that's a hopelessly reactionary fantasy.

How might you explain the natural talent that some people seem to have for writing—independent of any professional development that they may have as a writer?

I can't explain it. It just happens.

How do you think the human imagination generates the ideas that it does? Is imagination a mechanism of some cosmic

force that we cannot explain, or is it all produced in-house? By this I mean, do you think that the imagination is entirely the expression of one's nature and also nurture, or does it transcend such—a force inexplicable? For example, people independently coming up with the same ideas, often during the same period of time.

As with the previous reply.

How do you hope to be remembered in the field of science fiction?

As someone who wrote a lot of stories, some of which were pretty good and contributed to the overall body of science fiction.

What do you think your legacy in science fiction is?

See previous answer.

Is there another distinct and creative chapter planned for Bob Silverberg the bestselling and award-winning author, or is this a time now for enjoying the fruits of your literary labors and maybe growing some nice tomatoes?

We buy the tomatoes in the super-market. But I see no creative chapter ahead for me. As I said, it's time to rest. Willie Mays isn't playing baseball anymore and I'm not going to be writing stories in my 90s.

Are you concerned that new generations of science fiction fans may not be as familiar with your work as preceding generations? If so, why?

Things change. Nobody remembers such big names of the Thirties as Bob Olsen, David H. Keller, and Harl Vincent. Some of the important figures of the Forties are starting to fade from view. It will happen to me, too, but I won't be here to see it. I definitely want the new readers to know about my work, and here in my retirement years I work hard at keeping my science fiction visible in every format available.

How would you define science fiction? What elements must it contain?

I've been struggling with this business of definition for many decades now. I don't have a good answer. One definition of science fiction that I can offer is that I think it was much of what I wrote, but that's a retreat into tautology.

Do you think that science fiction can help to solve some of humanity's problems by generating ideas and building worldviews of the possible, or is SF somehow just window dressing on the human condition?

I suppose it can help, a little, to solve some of humanity's problems, but, judging by the way those problems seem to be piling up, it isn't doing a very good job.

Has persistence or inspiration been of more value to you in your writing career?

Of equal importance, I'd say.

Which book by Bob Silverberg should everyone read? Why?

A tough question. Some people define me by *Dying Inside*, some by *Lord Valentine's Castle*, and they are wildly different sorts of books that generate wildly different reactions from readers. I'd prefer not to make a choice here.

You've been a fan of science fiction for a very long time. Has it ever lost any of its shine for you?

Oh, yes. Of course it has. I've lived practically 90 years and just about everything has lost its shine for me. But I have no regrets about having devoted so much of my life to science fiction, even if it no longer gives me the jolt it did when I was fifteen.

Do you think that vitamin SF is the cognitive supplement we need to expand our thinking?

Definitely. Prepares us for what we were all calling "future shock" a generation or so ago.

Science fiction provides blueprints of the possible and the occasional flourish of wonder. As an element within the sphere of SF, does cynicism provide any benefits?

I don't have an answer for this one.

SF has been called the literature of ideas; it is also a collective thought experiment. Do you think we are leveraging these characteristics productively in advancing human potential?

As I said above, I don't think we can change the world through science fiction. We can stir some interesting speculations, though.

I've long thought that successful authors must enjoy a pleasant balance between celebrity and privacy. Have you found this to be the case?

Yes. I don't want my readers thronging my front door but I don't want to be ignored, either, and so I do make myself reasonably accessible through the Internet and at science-fiction conventions.

You have had various of your work published in Worlds of IF *decades ago. Now here we are again. What are your thoughts on that?* [Galaxy, *too, but when this interview was being conducted, I only asked about* Worlds of IF, *not being at all sure of the timeline for* Galaxy's *relaunch, but already having published the first issue of* Worlds of IF *with the second and third issues well underway.*]

I'm fascinated by the idea that *IF* is coming around again. I remember buying the first issues back in 1952, and thinking it was an extremely attractive magazine that I would love to see a story of mine in. (I wasn't ready yet, though.) Under the editorships of Larry Shaw and Damon Knight it ran a lot of superb stories that led me to look upon it as one of the best magazines of the field. And then, starting in 1956, I actually began selling stories to it, and kept on doing so for decades. I'm amazed to find that it's coming back here in the 21st century, and that I'm still around to write for it.

Do you think that the genre of science fiction has fully established itself in the grand constellation of literature?

I hope so.

Are you a fan of speculative poetry? How about very short forms like science fiction haiku?

I don't read much SF poetry. Eliot, Yeats, Matthew Arnold, yes. But they didn't do SF.

Please share your thoughts on AI, especially as it pertains to writing. [Since conducting this interview, the membership of the Science Fiction Poetry Association (SFPA) has voted, overwhelmingly, to prohibit the use of AI in the creation of the poetry and art submitted to them for publication and contests. I heartily applaud this result— and, in fact, voted for it.]

I haven't let myself get caught up in the AI frenzy. I'm aware that a lot of people are using it to write stories, but if I were writing these days myself I would try to do it only with whatever I was born with.

[Cover reveal!] The third issue of Worlds of IF *will feature spectacular cover art by Bruce Pennington which was in fact the cover art for your novel* The Man in the Maze, *originally serialized in the April and May 1968 issues of* Worlds of IF. *The novel takes an allegorical approach in its exploration of the individual in society. Please tell us about this story and your inspiration for writing it.*

I have long been interested in Greek tragedy, and while re-reading Sophocles's play *Philoctetes* I suddenly saw a way of telling that story as science fiction. I wrote the novel and sent it to Frederik Pohl with the idea that he would run it in *Galaxy*, which I regarded as the top-of-the-line magazine then, but Fred was trying to boost the popularity of his companion magazine *IF*, and used it there. It was very popular with the readers, and later on quite a few of my novels were serialized in *Galaxy*, so I reached that goal anyway. *Maze* has gone through quite a few editions over the years and is still in print. I think it would make a terrific movie, and for about fifteen years it was under option in Hollywood, but so far nothing has happened there with it.

Thank you, Bob! Here's to health and happiness!

Cheers,
Justin

COMING SOON!

A WERESHARK'S MEMOIR

A NOVELETTE

By

Justin T. O'Conor Sloane

In his magnum opus *Ethics* published posthumously in 1677, Spinoza argues that God is substance. Evil is substance in *A Wereshark's Memoir* by Justin Sloane. Original, frightening, and beautiful, this work is a study into the impossibility of evil to reign over the human race. It is a fiction of the open wound. It hurts and it makes you invent a therapy to alleviate pain. Often this is impossible. In a way, it is a subtle analysis of what society suffers from today. As Justin Sloane puts it, "Time is neither friend nor foe. But it can be made either."

EUGEN BACON is an African Australian author. She's a British Fantasy Award winner, a Foreword Indies Award winner, and twice World Fantasy Award finalist. Eugen was announced in the honor list of the Otherwise Fellowships for "doing exciting work in gender and speculative fiction." *Danged Black Thing* made the Otherwise Award Honor List as a "sharp collection of Afro-Surrealist work," and was a 2024 Philip K Dick Award nominee. Visit her at **eugenbacon.com**.

F. J. BERGMANN is the poetry editor of *Mobius: The Journal of Social Change* and freelances as a copy editor and book designer. She lives in Wisconsin and imagines tragedies on or near exoplanets. She is a Writers of the Future winner and the recipient of the 2024 SFPA Grand Master Award. Her work has appeared in *Asimov's SF, Analog, Polu Texni, Spectral Realms, Vastarien*, and elsewhere. She thinks imagination can compensate for anything.

ELIANE BOEY (she/her) is a Singaporean writer of speculative fiction, and a member of the SFWA, with stories in *Clarkesworld, the Penn Review, Weird Horror*, and others. Her latest book is *Club Contango* (Dark Matter INK, out in November 2024), a space-set murder mystery. Her previous work, *Other Minds*, is a duology of cyberpunk and space horror novellas. Online at **elianeboey.com**.

RONAN CAHILL lives and paints in Scotland. Exile, erosion of identity, imagined worlds, and particle physics are central themes. His work encompasses landscape, abstract, and digital spaces within which he can ask great questions of himself and in which lost worlds collide, are destroyed, and created. Ronan is a self-taught artist and has worked as an engineer for over 20 years. He believes that as artists, the only necessity is to show up at the tablet, page, or canvas – some creative force then takes charge. Ronan has drawn and painted all his life and is a member of Visual Arts Scotland. In 1997, he won first prize in the annual UCD Visual Arts Society exhibition. Online at **ronancahill.com**.

A J DALTON is a British fantasy writer and teacher of English. He is the author of the best-selling Chronicles of a Cosmic Warlord (*Empire of the Saviours, Gateway of the Saviours* and *Tithe of the Saviours*), the Flesh & Bone Series (*Necromancer's Gambit, Necromancer's Betrayal* and *Necromancer's Fall*), and three collections with Grimbold Books (*The Book of Orm, The Book of Angels* and *The Book of Dragons*). He has also published a range of academic articles on science fiction and fantasy. Dalton's academic study of fantasy and its subgenres was completed in 2018, when he completed a PhD with the University of Huddersfield. That academic work, his earlier publications and website (2008) have seen him recognized as the creator and lead author of the fantasy sub-genre known as "metaphysical fantasy." Online at **ajdalton.eu**.

BOB EGGLETON is a successful science fiction, fantasy and landscape artist. His art appears on the covers and in the interiors of numerous magazines and books. Bob is the winner of twelve Chesley Awards, nine Hugo Awards, two Locus Awards, and a Skylark Award. Bob's books include *Alien Horizons: The Fantastic Art of Bob Eggleton* (Paper Tiger/Dragon's World, 1995) with Nigel Suckling, *The Book of Sea Monsters* (Paper Tiger, 1998) with Nigel Suckling, and—the 2001 Hugo winner—*Greetings From Earth: The Art of Bob Eggleton* (Paper Tiger, 2000) with Nigel Suckling, *Dragonhenge* (Paper Tiger, 2002) with John Grant, *Primal Darkness: The Gothic & Horror Art of*

Bob Eggleton (Cartouche, 2003), *The Stardragons* (Paper Tiger, 2005) with John Grant, and *Dragons' Domain: The Ultimate Dragon Painting Workshop* (David & Charles, 2010). Bob has also worked as a conceptual illustrator for movies such as *Sphere* (1998), *Jimmy Neutron Boy Genius* (2001), and *The Ant Bully* (2006), and for the thrill ride STAR TREK THE EXPERIENCE in Las Vegas. Lately, he has been doing more animated movie concept work, private commissions, self-commissioned work and illustrated books. Bob has been elected as a Fellow of The International Association of Astronomical Artists (FIAAA) and is a Fellow of The New England Science Fiction Association (NESFA). He also appeared as a fleeing extra in the 2002 film *Godzilla Against Mechagodzilla*.

ZDRAVKA EVTIMOVA is a Bulgarian author whose short stories have been published in 32 countries. Her short story collections and novels have been published in the USA, UK, Canada, Italy, France, Greece, North Macedonia, Israel, Iran and China. Her short story "Blood" is included in an anthology of recommended readings for teaching literature in junior high schools in the USA and in the high school curriculum in Denmark. Her short story "Vassil," was one of ten award-winning stories in the BBC's 2005 worldwide short story competition, and her novel *The Arch* was nominated for the 2007 Book of Europe. Her literary awards include the 2000 Razvitie Literary Award for Best Bulgarian Contemporary Novel, 2003 Best Bulgarian Novel Award (Union of Bulgarian Writers), 2005 Anna Kamenova National Short Story Award, 2005 & 2010 Golden Necklace Best Short Story of the Year National Prize, 2014 Balkanika International Fiction Prize, 2015 Blaga Dimitrova National Fiction Prize, 2015 Best Novel of the Year National Award, 2017 Best Bulgarian Novel Award, 2020 Hristo Danov National Literary Award, and the 2022 Mihai Eminescu Prize for Fiction.

DAVID GERROLD is the author of over 50 books, hundreds of articles and columns, and over a dozen television episodes. He is a classic sci-fi writer that will go down in history as having created some of the most popular and redefining scripts, books, and short stories in the genre. TV credits include episodes from *Star Trek* ("The Trouble With Tribbles" and "The Cloud Minders"), *Star Trek Animated* ("More Tribbles, More Troubles" and "Bem"), *Babylon 5* ("Believers"), Twilight Zone ("A Day In Beaumont" and "A Saucer Of Loneliness"), *Land Of The Lost* ("Cha-Ka," "The Sleestak God," "Hurricane," "Possession," and "Circle"), *Tales From The Darkside* ("Levitation" and "If The Shoes Fit"), *Logan's Run* ("Man Out Of Time"), and others. Novels include *When HARLIE Was One, The Man Who Folded Himself, The War Against The Chtorr* septology, *The Star Wolf* trilogy, *The Dingilliad* young adult trilogy, the *Trackers* duology, and many more sci-fi classics. Additionally, the autobiographical tale of his son's adoption, *The Martian Child*, won the Hugo and Nebula awards for Best Novelette of the Year and was the basis for the 2007 movie *Martian Child*, starring John Cusack, Amanda Peet, and Joan Cusack. Online at **gerrold.com**.

RICHARD GRIECO is an actor, musician, artist, photographer, producer, director, and writer who has been wowing audiences with his performances and multigenre talent since *21 Jump Street*. Online at **richardgrieco-official.com**.

RODNEY MATTHEWS was trained at the West of England College of Art, working in advertising for Plastic Dog

Graphics before turning freelance in 1970, initially under the name Skyline Studios. He has painted over 140 subjects for record album covers, for many high-profile rock and progressive rock bands. More than 90 of his pictures have been published worldwide, selling in poster format, as well as many international editions of calendars, jigsaw puzzles, postcards, notecards, snowboards and T-shirts. His originals have been exhibited throughout the UK and Europe. He was a regular exhibitor at the Chris Beetles Gallery, in London's West End, where he met John Cleese, an avid collector of his work. Matthews has illustrated numerous books, including those of Michael Moorcock. Their collaboration in the 1970s resulted in a series of 12 large posters, depicting scenes from Moorcock's Eternal Champion series, also used for a 1978 calendar, "Wizardry and Wild Romance." In 1998, Matthews and the late Gerry Anderson completed *Lavender Castle*, a 26-episode stop-motion/CG television series for children. Matthews also contributed concept designs for the 2005 film *The Magic Roundabout*. He supplied conceptual designs for computer games such as the Sony/Psygnosis game *Shadow Master* and *Haven: Call of the King*, published by Midway. Matthews has also produced publicity and a logo for the green energy company Ecotricity. He has written lyrics and played drums on a music album influenced by his images. Online at **rodneymatthewsstudios.com**.

BRUCE PENNINGTON is an internationally acclaimed artist working in the genres of science fiction and fantasy. He has created the cover art for more than 200 books by the biggest names in the industry. Visit **brucepennington.co.uk** to see more of the work that has defined the field of science fiction since his covers for Herbert's *Dune* series awed readers fifty years ago.

DR. DANIEL POMARÈDE is a staff scientist at the Institute of Research into the Fundamental Laws of the Universe, CEA Paris-Saclay University. He co-discovered Laniakea, our home supercluster of galaxies, and Ho'oleilana, a spherical shell-like structure 1 billion light-years in diameter found in the distribution of galaxies, possibly the remnant of a Baryon Acoustic Oscillation. Specialized in data visualization and cosmography, a branch of cosmology dedicated to mapping the Universe, he also co-authored the discoveries of the Dipole Repeller and of the Cold Spot Repeller, two large influential cosmic voids, and the discovery of the South Pole Wall, a large-scale structure located in the direction of the south celestial pole beyond the southern frontiers of Laniakea. He graduated from the Interuniversity Magister degree in Physics of the Ecole Normale Supérieure de Paris and Paris Universities (1991–1994), training in diverse research projects: experimental atomic physics in the group led by Marie-Anne Bouchiat at Kastler–Brossel Laboratory, waveguide optics at the Laser Research Group, University of Manchester, supersymmetry at CEA Theoretical Physics Department in Saclay. He served overseas as a national service scientific cooperant at Brookhaven National Laboratory in New York and received a Master of Science degree from the University of South Carolina, contributing to the preparation and analysis of nuclear physics experiments on the spin structure of the nucleon. In 1999, Daniel completed his PhD in particle physics and cosmology at the Laboratoire de Physique Nucléaire des Hautes Energies at Ecole Polytechnique with a thesis on the search for cosmological antimatter in TeV cosmic rays, using the 10m Imaging Atmospheric Cerenkov Telescope at the F. L. Whipple Observatory in Arizona. He then held postdoctoral positions at CEA Service de Physique des Particules in Saclay and at the Physics Department of the University of Rome, La Sapienza, to work on the preparation of the ATLAS Experiment at CERN. In Saclay, he co-founded in 2005 the COAST Computational Astrophysics Program dedicated to supercomputer simulations in astronomy, in the context of which he developed the SDvision Saclay Data Visualization software. As of 2010 he is applying these data visualization and analysis techniques in the field of cosmography.

GARETH L. POWELL is the author of 20 published books. He is best known for *The Embers of War* trilogy, *The Continuance* series, the *Ack-Ack Macaque* trilogy, *Light Chaser* (written with Peter F. Hamilton), and *About Writing*, his guide for aspiring authors. He has twice won the British Science Fiction Association Award for Best Novel (previous winners include J. G. Ballard and Arthur C. Clarke) and has become one of the most shortlisted authors in the award's 50-year history. He has also been a finalist for the Locus Award, the British Fantasy Award, the Seiun Award, and the Canopus Award. He can be found online at **garethlpowell.com**.

CHRISTOPHER RUOCCHIO is the internationally award-winning author of the *Sun Eater*, a series blending elements of both science fiction and fantasy, as well as more than twenty works of short fiction. A graduate of North Carolina State University, he sold his first novel, *Empire of Silence*, at twenty-two, and his books have appeared in seven languages. He curated several short story anthologies for Baen Books, including *Sword & Planet*. His work has also appeared in Marvel Comics. Christopher lives in Raleigh, North Carolina with his family. Online at **sollanempire.com**.

PAULO SAYEG was born in 1960, in São Paulo, Brazil and has been involved with art since a child, learning painting and lithography from his uncle, Alberto Garutti. At 22 years old, Paulo presented a solo exhibition, the first of many, both domestic and international. Paulo continues to live in São Paulo, where he works in illustration, animation, visual programming and advertising. In 1987, the São Paulo Association of Art Critics (APCA) recognized Paulo with the award for best designer. APCA was established in 1956 and celebrates the best in the Brazilian fields of stage acting, music, literature, film, television, plastic arts, and radio.

ROBERT SILVERBERG is an American author and editor, best known for writing science fiction. He is a multiple winner of both Hugo and Nebula Awards, a member of the Science Fiction and Fantasy Hall of Fame, and a Grand Master of SFWA. He has attended every Hugo Award ceremony since the inaugural event in 1953. His many notable works include the novella *Nightwings* (1969) and the novels *Downward to the Earth* (1970), *The World Inside* (1971), *Dying Inside* (1972), and *Lord Valentine's Castle* (1980).

NIGEL SUCKLING is the author of more than twenty books and a bestselling tarot card with guidebook set, *The Dragon Tarot*. He is the winner of a Hugo Award and has collaborated with some of the biggest names in science fiction and fantasy in creating biographical, literary and artistic genre masterpieces. Visit **unicorngarden. com** for a magical expedition through the many decades of his splendid work.

DAVE VESCIO is an internationally award-winning contemporary artist and retired film star, having appeared in the films *Hick*, *Gemini Rising* and many others. See more of his work at **davevescio.com**.

Heroes are not always what they seem

EMPIRE
OF THE
SAVIOURS

A. J. DALTON

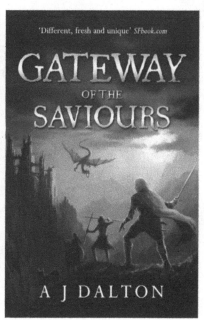

'Different, fresh and unique' *SFbook.com*

GATEWAY
OF THE
SAVIOURS

A J DALTON

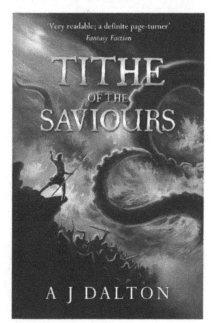

'Very readable; a definite page-turner'
Fantasy Faction

TITHE
OF THE
SAVIOURS

A J DALTON

**Read
the complete
Cosmic Warlord
trilogy
by A J Dalton
on Amazon
now!**

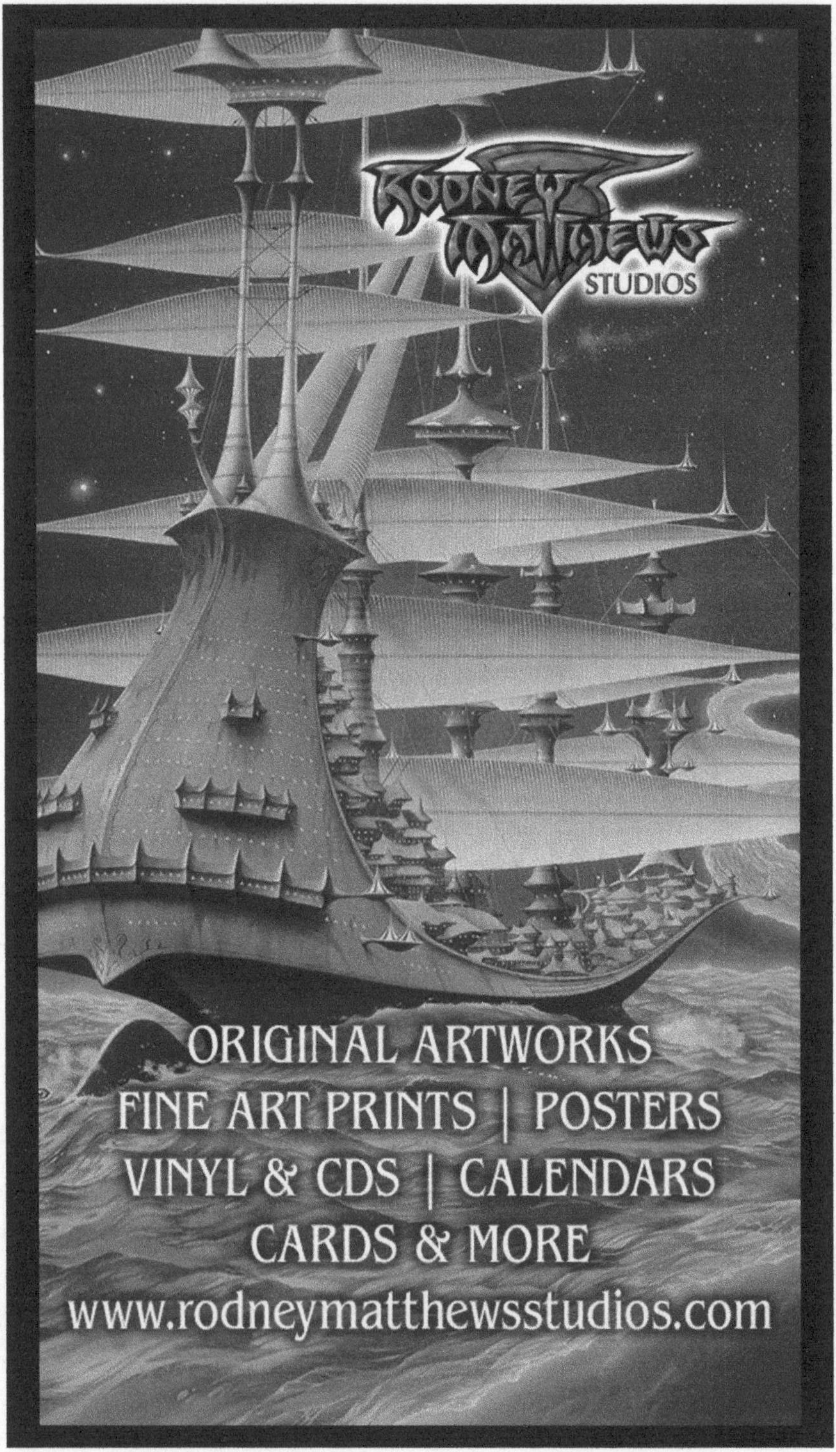
RODNEY MATTHEWS
STUDIOS
ORIGINAL ARTWORKS
FINE ART PRINTS | POSTERS
VINYL & CDS | CALENDARS
CARDS & MORE
www.rodneymatthewsstudios.com